D1523746

ISBN-13: 9781434848321
ISBN-10: 1434848329

Cover design by: Create Space
Library of Congress Control Number: 2015900301
Printed in the United States of America

Dedicated to

Mom, Dad, Doug, Alex and Cole

(the order I met you all)

GOODBYE DEF LEPPARD
(I'LL MISS THOSE JEANS)

BY
STEF KRAMER

Present Day

Joyful.

Joyful. Joyful.

I repeat the word to myself.

Last night my kids all agreed I took the happy out of everything. Their words trembled in the air as I pictured myself through their eyes, my expression scrutinizing the flour-caked kitchen—a valiant attempt at sugar cookies. Had I ramped into more monster than mother? I wanted to explain my reaction, as they stood sullen-faced, their glee stolen away by the person they wanted to impress. How could they possibly understand the stress of a workday? How it will consume unsuspecting portions of emotional energy, making seemingly trivial events, like a messy kitchen, monumental? I felt awful. Even with my tired apologies, I had ruined the evening.

I gave myself a pep talk today. What kind of mom do I want to be? At the very least, one who greets her kids with a smile. So today I'm determined to walk through the door with a positive perspective, no matter what I encounter.

"Mother Fudger," I grunt, tripping over the mound of shoes in the doorway, a cat daring to escape, and a bouncing terrier with a need to slobber on my face. I take a deep, cleansing breath, and sing out, "Hellooo! How are my babies?"

No response. I only hear the whiny voice of Squidword lecturing through our kitchen TV. The boys are sitting at the breakfast bar, riveted to the screen. I sneak up and kiss the top of their sweaty, somewhat rakish hair.

"Mommy!" They say in nearly perfect unison.

I hug my twins, eyeing the Pringle crumbs and pools of juice on the counter.

"Where's your sister?" I ask.

They shrug, unable to converse with me, lest they miss a crucial moment of Spongebob.

"Did she make you a snack after school?"

Cole waves an empty Pringle's canister.

Quinn turns to me, looking up with his impish brown eyes. "More please."

"How about some carrots? Healthy and delicious."

"Gross," says Cole, his perk nose replaced by a dubious wrinkle.

An ounce of joyful has slipped away.

I set out the baby carrots anyway. After a thirty-second wait with no takers, I give in. A bag of Doritos finds its way between my sons.

Clipping through the house, I call out for Marra. The dog is on my heels. I wonder if she has remembered to feed him. Two ounces of joy: gone.

"Mom!" She calls from the top of the stairs.

"Right here."

"Get down here. Now. Please."

She races down the stairs, and I am taken aback by the whirl of hair and array of pink fabric before me. A color bomb has landed in our home.

"How do I look?" She asks flipping about her boisterous curls.

An oversized shirt, acid-washed-ripped jeans, and mesh fingerless gloves speak to me from a distant land, as if my daughter has just hitched a ride from 1988.

"Been scavenging in the storage room?" I ask, now kneeling to pet the slobbering dog.

"Huh?"

"The jeans? Where'd you find them?"

"Uh, bought these with Gracie and her mom last weekend at Hot Topic. Remember? I told you. Got 'em especially for the concert tonight!"

Vaguely remembering the conversation, I approach my daughter studying the ridges of the washed-out denim, feeling the vulnerability of the fray. I lift her hands to inspect the neon gloves. "And these? Where'd you find–"

"Guess."

"Perhaps I've judged Hot Topic too harshly."

She nods, in her big, know-it-all way.

The dog scratches at me, as I stand up straight, considering my daughter's look.

"Homework status?" I ask.

"Done."

"Have you practiced?"

"On my way."

"Feed the dog food first," I instruct, starting up the stairs. "I'll be down in a few."

Ten minutes later, I strut into our dining room wearing another pair of acid-washed, tattered jeans. (My shirt hides the fact I can't quite get them buttoned.)

My daughter halts her piano practice, hands flying to her face. "Ohmygod...no."

"In a galaxy far, far away, these fit me much better."

The boys shift their attention from the breakfast nook, then burst into giggle. My daughter drops her head on a trove a muddled keys, but I sense a smile under that head of hair.

"Why'd you keep them all these years?" She says with her head still laying on the piano. Then her head pokes up. "Were you wearing them when you met Dad? Or when he saved you from ending up with that one guy who was a–"

"These jeans have nothing to do with your father," I say a bit sharper then I intend. Marra's eyes shift to that special hue of teenage stone and I realize she's misconstrued my tone. "Sorry. But some of my relics have nothing to do with your dad. I'm not even sure I ever wore these particular jeans around him."

The boys are back to Spongebob. But my daughter is staring at me, as if she's waiting for more story. At fourteen perhaps she's reaching the age of romantic notions.

"Keep practicing, baby," I say. "I need to offer up some socks to the washing machine before we leave."

I start toward the utility room when Marra turns on the bench to ask, "Will you listen to me, Mom? Please? Contest is coming up."

Piano contest. This Saturday. The instrument makes her nervous.

I calculate the number of socks and underwear the kids have for the week, and how long it might take me to listen through her repertoire. Then laughter from the kitchen interrupts my thoughts, knocking my blurred vision to focus on Marra's pretty face who's waiting for a response.

"Of course, baby," I say. "I'd love to.

Her face lifts from a small shadow. She sets her sheet music aside and arranges her hands on the keys as I nestle into the bay window nook–my spot to monitor our backyard and keep myself apprised of the changing tapestry of the seasons. The view is inhabited by a brick fire pit, designed by my husband, but hardly ever used. I wonder if I ever told him how lovely I think it is.

As my daughter counts herself into a Mozart Sonata, I lay my head back, taking in the spirited music and the view. The sky teeters between blue and green – as if it can't decide, kind of like a smile that's not quite happy and not quite sad. I shift back to my daughter, whose unflinching gaze of the keyboard couldn't possibly allow one beat to escape her.

Technically, she plays nearly to perfection, without missing a note, rhythm, or a crescendo as composed. Yet, as I listen, I detect a robotic quality in the performance – a disconnect from emotion. Perhaps this will come.

The trills. The melodic runs. I sit up, leaning toward the piano, moving my fingers along, aching to play along. Then before me, appears Cole, holding out my phone.

"It's dinging like crazy, Mommy."

He drops the phone in my lap, and trudges away. Marra stops playing, guilting me with a glare while the ding of work emails beckon me. Always, it seems, I'm caught between.

"Can't you leave work alone," she snaps. "For two seconds."

I didn't go after my phone. It was served to me by my son. Still, my daughter observes my sudden shift from her performance as I consider issues needing my attention at work.

My attention.

I power down my phone and set it on the far side of the window.

"My apologies, pretty girl," I say. "Please. Carry on."

"How do I sound?" She looks down, tapping her hands on the bench.

"Good. Really good."

"But?"

"But what?" I ask.

"I'm sure you have suggestions."

"Hardly any," I say. "You might've rushed in a few spots. I can tell you like the quick-pace, so it wouldn't hurt to use the metronome. And try imagining something when you play, so you feel more connected."

She purses her lip.

"But overall, I thought it to be superior." I get up, stepping toward Marra to kiss the top of her head. "Can I hear you sing?"

She nods. "I'll sing you my pops concert stuff."

"Need me to accompany you?"

"Nah," she says. "It's easier this way."

My girl plays the first few chords of a Katie Perry, then opens her voice up to the melody. She scoops into notes, and exaggerates her runs. But her tone is spring-water clear. I feel myself grow numb. Her voice is silk. So silk. I linger for a moment, then sit next to her on the bench.

Now she's passionate. Engaged. And she's pushing me into a state of emotion that borders on wistful, but is probably better described as nostalgic. I can identify with the joy in her projection. The sense of wholeness, when lyrics and pitch and emotion transcend to sublime. She's feeling it. I'm feeling it.

I step back over to the window, sinking into the cushions as my daughter's voice floats about the room. What she couldn't do with that voice. I knew a voice like that once. A voice that somehow transformed into something more like a Siri app. But more bossy.

Glancing down, I begin to pick at a rip in my jeans. How *did* I get to this place in my life? This place of constant, internal struggle? This place that has me all wound up, lashing out, and projecting some persona I don't recognize, nor really like?

Maybe I'd find the answer to that question if I knew why I left behind what I left behind.

CHAPTER 1

IOWA CITY, COLLEGE TOWN

MAY 1992

I focus a steady eye on the artsy purple bubble around today's date on my Simpson's calendar.

Graduation day. Sort of.

Sitting on the edge of my bed, with the clamor of train cars banging outside my window, I'm experiencing a touch of paralysis. I glance around my room of dirty laundry and books. Scant belongings to pack. White walls with two posters. The Nutcracker Ballet and Led Zeppelin. A slightly frayed purple quilt. My hole.

I convince myself up to cross out the square designating the ninth of May. Every day before this, I've counted down with an undaunted confidence, only considering how my homework would be folding up. Now, this image of Bart Simpson's sadistic smile fails to entertain me.

I'm moving home for the summer, where expectations lurk and a boy from my past dodges about.

The frenetic energy I shared with my roommate three hours ago, as we slipped home from the bars to indulge in a Domino's pizza, has been devoured by the sunlight and my glum spirit. We giggled through our double-cheese, analyzing the events of our evening. She attributed my decline in dance partners to my special face framing move. I promised to brush up on my Madonna. "Just because you can sing Amy Gaer," she said, "doesn't mean you can dance."

I hoist myself up, and plod to our kitchenette. My unlaundered sweat-infused workout attire immediately confronts a lemony fresh scent of Pine Sol.

"Been scrubbing this morning?" I ask, fitting a walkman over my ears ready for the toxic lyrics of Guns N Roses to blast into my slightly fuzzy brain.

"Seriously? Jogging?" Jean is dressed only in her bra and panties, ironing zealously at her graduation attire. "You *are* insane. Bet you feel like shit."

With a pronounced sniff of the air, I utter, "We all have our neurotic tendencies. What time did Mr. Clean show up?" I sidle up to Jean, wrapping my arm around her. "I'm sad. It's the end. Margarita and B-movie night. Boy-scouting in the library. Open-mic night at College Street."

"You'll be back next semester. No one's stopping you from partaking in those activities."

It won't be the same! Don't leave me for your fancy job in Chicago!

Grabbing her mortar cap, I attempt to arrange it over my headphones.

"How do I look?"

She raises her eyes and drops her head to the side. "Like a typical Liberal Arts graduate. Ungrounded."

"Business majors. Assholes."

"Candid," she says, inspecting her dress for wrinkles. "I prefer the term 'candid.' Maybe you'll develop that most awesome characteristic once you capture that finance degree. Dump the English major bit."

"I *am* an English major, if you recall. That's my degree as of today, you know."

She shrugs, with her eyes.

"And I should be going to law school," I say. "It's your fault I missed the LSATs. That's what I tell my mom anyway."

"Blame me all you want for your nocturnal festivities, but you can't blame me for failing to show up the entrance exams. Three times!" She reaches over to our wobbly table, where I sit, and pats my cheek. "Promise me something, will ya? No more music classes this fall?"

Six hours short of a music minor. No promises.

I double-tie my tennis shoes before boosting myself up, cheering myself on for the jog.

"As a matter of fact," Jean says, "if you get the

sudden urge to start loitering around symphonies or choir concerts, step directly to Blockbuster and rent *Working Girl* again." She drops her dress to the floor, even though she just ironed it, then pulls my face to her. "Let's show corporate America how savvy small town Iowa girls can be. And kill it in our Burberry suits."

Slipping on her black dress, Jean looks like she just stepped out of Vogue magazine. Tall. Curly-red hair. She's Julia Roberts, without the toothy smile. Not sure why I like my roommate so much, except she makes me laugh.

As I stretch for my jog, she pulls a small box out of a drawer. Tossing it to me she says, "Got ya a little something."

"What?" I say, my mind suddenly in a lurch about a gift for her. "I haven't had a chance to wrap–"

"When I said little, I meant little. Just open it."

I tear open the package to find a three-legged pig carved of wood.

"It's supposed to bring you good fortune. I know how you like all that superstitious shit. And how you might need some luck this summer."

Her voice trails off because she knows my dread. I'm touched by her concern. Even though she's not watching me, I smile directly at her. "I love it, roomy-pal."

I tap my forehead, inducing it to think. Then I make my way back to my bedroom, as she shouts out, "I don't want any of your hand-medowns." Staring around the room, I spot two of my other three-legged pigs. I push them deeply into my dresser, before I land my eyes on a ragged edition of *Poems* by Emily Dickenson, Series One. She'll hate it.

I scribble a note in the cover before bouncing back to the kitchen.

"For you, my friend."

She looks at me blankly. "When's this due back to the library?"

I shake my head, then open the cover and point to my inscription which she reads aloud.

"Time never will assuage. Find your poetry. Ever Yours, A."

She raises one thick eyebrow at me. "That's too deep for me."

"I know." I turn to leave for my jog, while adjusting my headphones. Before walking out the door, I shout, "This sucks."

I glance behind me, but Jean has gone to the bathroom to primp for the graduation ceremony today. Not saying goodbye seems apropos for now.

As I step out of our apartment complex, I take a deep breath and consider my route.

CHAPTER 2
NEVER SAY GOODBYE

MAY 1992

For now, my hometown anxiety takes a backseat as I take a final tour of Iowa City.

The shrieking of Slash's guitar escalate my pace as *Welcome to the Jungle* numbs my ears. The traffic on Gilbert Street revs with a peaceful excitement—as if the cars are chattering about the fun from last night, gearing up for another. Like much of the student populace, the busy streets can't wait for the sun to go down even though it's hardly begun to make its ascent.

Upon reaching the pedestrian mall, I slow to walk on jagged brick, past the shops on Dubuque Street to find myself standing before the gray, unassuming facade of Prairie Lights Bookstore. It's easy to be distracted by the emerald Irish pub next door known as Mickey's. Either these businesses are strategic alliances or fierce competitors.

Stepping into the store, a hint of coffee and aged vellum encompass me. To think, on my first visit here, I was a bit put off by the starkness and vacuum of silence. Completely unlike the obnoxious campus bookstore. That was before my friend, Paul, acclimated me into this literary haven. Now, I crave it. I love the pseudo-famous author readings. More so than the famous author readings. I love reading through the staff picks and trying to decipher the meaning of their inflated vocabulary. I love skimming the first half of classics written by Jane Austen or Charles Dickens. Of course, Paul tells me those novels are practically grade school curriculum. I could do better as an English major, he says.

For a moment, my eyes become bleary, taking in a moment. Then I spot my target hunched over the back counter in his signature black t-shirt. His studious expression helps me transition past my sentiment.

"Are you really working?" I ask. "Or just penning away on your novel?"

"What are we listening to today?" says my friend, feverishly writing on a notepad while holding his hand in a page of *Cry, the Beloved Country*. "Motley Crue?"

"Not today." I post up with my elbows before him. "Axl Rose. Even his name is pure poetry."

"I have The Cure in my pack," he says without looking up. "And I'll be taking out the trash soon if you'd like to hand over that crap in your walkman."

"I wouldn't deprive you. And what would happen if I took the tape back to Loam County? I'd be ostracized." Paul glances at me with his pretty sky-blue eyes and unnaturally black hair. "That would be tragic."

"Tragic."

"Better keep listening to your trashy metal."

"You know it."

Putting down his pencil, Paul massages his hands. After a deep yawn, he says, "You perplex me, Amy Gaer. One moment you're banging your head. Then I find out you're spending Friday night at the opera." He tilts his head. "One minute you're studying literature, talking about law school. The next minute you're embracing Wall Street."

Paul picks up his unsharpened pencil and begins to write again.

"A staff pick?" I ask.

He nods.

"Isn't that book kind of old?"

"I was going to review *Ishmael*. Daniel Quinn."

I nod as if I know what book he's referring to. Then Paul squints over to the clerk at one of the other checkouts. "But Paris already did. Don't bother to read her awful synopsis. I doubt we'll sell a single copy now. Thought I'd try something different than choose something right off the press."

I think back to the time we met. Second semester. Sophomore year. I introduced myself as we waited for our professor to arrive for our in-depth study of Hamlet. When he told me his name was Paul Rogers, I tried to be coy by asking him if he was the lead singer of Bad Company.

"That guy's probably dead," he said. "And I'm gay. No need to bother with me."

What *did* make me bother with him? Perhaps I thought I could break through that surly personality. Perhaps I was naive. Nevertheless, I was determined to be his friend, for some reason. And I still am.

A book teeters on the edge of a table nearby. Grabbing it I ask, "Could you help me with a few light reading picks? Stuff to immerse me while I'm home this summer?" I flash him the copy in my hand. Edith Wharton's *House of Mirth*. "This sounds happy. What d'ya think?"

His eyes drift between the book and my face. "It's perfect."

I thumb through the pages. "Wait! Is she the same author who wrote that one book with the sleigh ride and the crippled woman?"

Paul places a marker in his book before addressing me. "Amy, I do think a business degree will serve you well."

I sense my friend does not mean this as a compliment.

"However," he continues, "may I offer something for you to consider?"

I stand up, struck by my friend's sudden attention toward me. This will either be a snowball or a dozen roses.

"You're a musician. Pretty talented, from my amateur perspective. Keep honing those skills." Paul sips on a coffee as I shake off his comments. "Really Amy. Not everyone gets solos in a college choir."

One solo. One small solo. Too small for the more invested students.

"Maybe business is the right channel for you," he says as I look down, thinking about his comment. "But I'm very intuitive. And something tells me you should continue your musical pursuits."

"No rock band wanted me as their lead singer, remember?"

A customer interrupts us by tapping Paul on his sleeve, asking him a question. Paul holds a finger to me, while listening to his newest challenge involving a short story collection of Kate Chopin. After ten minutes that has moved way beyond Kate Chopin, I realize the customer has no intention of ending his discussion with Paul.

I wave goodbye, but Paul acts like he doesn't see me. As I move to leave with the Edith Wharton still in my hand, Paul stops me. "Paying for that?"

"Oh!" I say, "I forgot to bring money."

For a few moments, Paul, his customer, and I are statues. Then his customer asks, "So does that work? You tell the store you forgot your money, and they let you take it?"

Setting the book down, I whisper, "Bye."

With his smirky, forced grin, he nods once before turning away.

I leave the bookstore with my heart pumping faster than when I was at full stride. Not only am I embarrassed, but I have unfinished business. My plan was to remind Paul about writing me from New York City, especially when he met someone famous. Oh well. There's a decent chance he won't think about me after today anyway. Even though he seeps into my mind all the time. I have this thing about loners. I worry.

My jog resumes, and I snake my way through the towering buildings on the Pentacrest, down the hill to race along side the murky Iowa River. The smell of the river washes out the linen of the spring air. It's a perfect complement to the old granite lecture halls which now look so deserted.

Paul's words play over in my mind. *You're a musician.* To do what? Teach? And not really make anything of myself?

I meet other jogging students on the sidewalk. Our stranger eyes meet, and we exchange sad parting smiles to mark the end of the school year. I pass some students sitting on the river bank, gazing over the water. Some toss bread out to the intrepid ducks, maybe for the last time.

No local rock band would take me. Didn't get one call back. So, what's that tell me? I'm not good enough to make it as a performer. Doesn't matter anyway. Like my mother has always said, dreaming like that's never gonna get me anywhere.

But.

Here I am.

Standing in front of the music building. Dwarfed by the overhanging edifice of Hancher's Auditorium.

After I slip into one of the practice rooms which happened to be unlocked, I position myself on the bench of a lustrous, black Yamaha. My dream machine. The room next to me pounds with the fever of Bach. I block it out with a few scales to loosen my fingers. The lightness of the keys make me content to fly through arpeggios for the next thirty or so minutes. And then I relax into the song I have sworn off so many times before. Journey's *Faithfully*. It always comes back, from my high school vocal days. My voice croons over the notes as my fingers flourish upon the keys. The room, filled with me and my ballad, transforms into a stage. I'm wearing a sequined evening gown, singing out to a stadium crowd, mesmerized by my performance.

A knock on the door stops me in mid-note.

I'm caught. My concert is over. Only music majors allowed in the rooms. No music major would sing pop songs here.

"Found you."

I swivel to see Mitch, perspiring an aura of rum and smoke. His disheveled, pompadour bangs give him the appearance of a punk rocker. Since he's not into hair products, I'm guessing his current likeness has been induced by a night of excess and lack of sleep.

"Why in the world would you be looking for me?" I stand up to grab his swaying shoulders.

"To give you flowers for graduation!" He looks down at his hands. "But I don't have the flowers. Is that okay?"

"You should be getting ready for the pomp and circumstance, my dear friend." I lead him to the piano bench to sit. "And how'd you know I'd be here?"

He puts his arm around me. "I knew 'xactly where you'd be. Cuz I'm smart. And Jean said you were out jogging."

I nod, amazed by his inebriated, circuitous path. "You need to get ready, dude."

"*You* need to get ready, dude."

"I'll attend the ceremony next semester."

"Amy?" Mitch says, with his head in an increasingly drooping state. "I'm gonna ask you one more time–"

"No."

"Thought I'd check."

"I still love you though," I say. "And just because I won't marry you, doesn't mean I can't wait to see you next fall. I know you'll probably have to study a little harder in grad school. But maybe you won't party so much. More my speed."

"Amy, love of my life, I haven't told you yet, but I'm leaving Iowa City. Northwestern accepted me. I'm startin' in their School of Education and Social Policy. Sounds important, doesn't it?"

Did he just say something about Northwestern? And leaving?

The piano next door plays a brisk movement, in a happy key, something completely disparate of my personal soundtrack right now.

"Oh," is all I manage to say, wondering who will even be around next semester to conjure up some sort of a social life. After I realize I'm chewing my lip and he's just staring at me, I muster up some words. "Mitch, that's awesome. Congratulations."

"Not as dumb as I look?"

"I'm feeling like the dumb one."

"Are you feeling sentimental about me?" He pulls his arms around me, then plants one on the lips. "Are you sure you won't marry me?"

"I'm reconsidering. Maybe we should date a little first."

"It's not like I haven't tried," he says.

I lay my head on his shoulder. "I'll miss you, Mitchie. Thanks for teaching me all the great party tricks."

"Brian and I will be around for awhile this summer. Don't be a stranger."

I shake my head, then kiss him on the cheek. We stare at each other. Lingering.

"Before I go, sing me a song?"

I look at the clock on the wall.

"Tell you what?" I say. "Let's sing a song to-

gether on the way out so you're not late for graduation."

"A duet?"

I close up the piano, pulling up my friend to
drag him out of the music building.

"Take my lead, because you really do need to
Busta Move." Facing Mitch, I shape my hands in front
of my face. "But I can only sing this if I do some face-
framing moves. It goes well with the beat."

"I'm witcha."

We rap together, Mitch struggling to keep up
with the lyrics. As we finish our homage to Young
MC, I put Mitch on a Cambus enroute to his apartment. He watches me out the window, fist in the air,
as if we just left a rock concert.

I head back to Gilbert Street, this time skip-
ping the view of the river, in favor of a more resi-
dential scene of the President's manor and other
stately homes with plushy grass on the east side of
campus. But the houses and signs become blurred as
I increase my speed. And then something happens.
The ground most definitely shifts from underneath
me as I cross the walking bridge to my apartment. I
stop at once, heart palpitating, to let this moment of
the end sink in. Just then I see it. A piece of copper
shining on the ground. Grabbing the penny without
looking to see which face is up, I squeeze it tightly in
my hand. Then bending over, arms wrapped around
myself, eyes closed, I do something I rarely do.

I pray.

Dear God. Help me to figure it out. I just want to be super successful and not disappoint my parents. Especially my mom. Thank you very much. Amen. Amy.

Nick's Journal

MAY 2, 1992

It's a beautiful day. Mid-70's. Hardly any wind. A good day to plant beans. Apparently, a good day to leave your husband as well.

I have no wife, no dog, no couch.

But I have an old kitchen table with a broken leg and a hundred year-old house that's painted half yellow. Canary yellow. I hate yellow.

I sit here in the storage room attic with a six-pack as my supper watching the last purple shreds of the sun, writing in my journal for the first time since forever. Scratching my head. Thinking.

Two years. Hardly long enough to give it a real chance. Maybe we just need some time apart. Or, maybe we were just too young. Or maybe I just didn't try hard enough.

Digging through my trunk I found the jade neck-lace Uncle Cal gave to me the day we all sat around his bedroom as he was dying. I was surprised when he told me to look for a pouch under that pile of blankets. When I found it, I assumed he'd tell me to hand it over to Mom, but he didn't. He said, "Give it to someone special. Before she gets away." I always wonder if Uncle Cal was thinking about his girlfriend who married someone else before he got back from WWII.

Someone special. Maybe it would've saved our marriage.

Maybe it still can.

CHAPTER 3

HOME

MAY 1992

So my summer begins.

"I'm not ready."

The weep in my mother's voice unnerves me as I sit at the old oak kitchen table, thumbing through the Sunday paper, spooning cereal milk into my coffee. The mood isn't typical for her. I wonder how long this particular issue has vexed her.

"But Kate. The house is a tomb," says my father as he grabs the business section I was pretending to read. "It's eerie. We need a dog."

"Amy's here now. Can't we just enjoy her? She is our only child."

I eke out a smile, nodding toward my dad. Although, I *am* curious about my mother's choice of words. Did she really mean to say, "enjoy her?"

"She's no dog," says my dad.

I turn to Mom. "He has a point. I don't do

tricks."

Mom's not amused. She remains at the sink, scrubbing a pan that has most likely been spotless for the last fifteen minutes. Not that I wasn't sad when when Dad called me to say Mitzi had died. But that was six months ago. I've moved on. My mother is still grieving.

"Alright," Dad says, watching my mother from the corner of his eye. "We can discuss later." Then he folds his hands together to face me. "So Amos. What's your plan this summer? Sponge off us? Or, you going back to the fields?"

The comment throws me back to the last time I came home to live with my parents. That summer of waiting tables, extricating Chris out of my life, and detasseling corn. *De-tasseling*. Trudging through tall corn fields, cutting tassels off the stalks, fighting insects, soiling my shoes, barely getting a tan since the corn was so tall. It was the hardest labor I ever did, so referred to myself as "Olan" from Pearl S. Buck's *The Good Earth*. No one got my joke, of course, because I'm certain no one on my crew ever read that book. Probably a good thing too, because comparing myself to a woman who can give birth and labor in the fields in the same day might've come across as a bit self-aggrandizing.

"Now Curt," I say to Dad in my adult voice. "I've got my liberal arts degree. Should I have to work in the fields or at a diner?"

"And that degree means you can pay me rent

as well?" Dad shoots back.

"How about I check out the cafe tomorrow?"

At least that job offered an amazing perk: unlimited, gargantuan, deep-fat fried rolls.

"When are you planning on telling her?" Mom joins us at the table.

"Tell me what?" I ask shifting around in my seat, somewhat excited that my parents have something–anything–to tell me.

Dad scratches his chin, as if he's deliberating. "Rick mentioned the Loam County Bank is looking for a summer teller. Maybe start something like a management trainee program. He gave the president your name when I mentioned you'd be home for the summer. Call him tomorrow if you're interested."

"Thank God for Rick Dawson and his connections!" I'm unable to hold back a smile. Dad goes back to reading the paper while Mom sips on her coffee."Did you say a 'management trainee program'?"

"He's probably glorifying the title to fill a position," says my mother. "I heard someone quit."

"Well I like the idea of a management trainee program. Sounds important. Even progressive for Fox Plaine. Maybe we'll get an ATM in town!"

"We have three ATMs, Miss Smarty Pants. This town isn't completely backward."

"Of course not." I stand up and give my mother a hug. "I'll call Mr. Bank president first thing tomorrow."

The possibility of adding "banking" on the experience part of my resume sounds fancy. Like my first real step towards entering the business world. And procuring an Audi.

After dumping my horrible cereal milk coffee, I grab a stack of Mom's magazines and check out the tanning weather on the deck to catch up on the latest vanity tips from Glamour and Cosmo. Faulkner and Calculus have taken too much of my time lately.

I position myself on my parents' deck so the sun's rays hit every possible piece of exposed skin. My ears are attuned for train cars colliding, but I only hear the chirping of the sparrow, and the whirling of a breeze. I'm unable to detect a single vehicle hum through the street of our homogenous ranch style houses, which is fine with me today. I let the environment relax into my bones with a certain ease. Perhaps the pace of our population of 5,000 won't be the worst thing in the world right now.

Let's hope.

CHAPTER 4

HIT ME LIKE A BOMB

MAY 1992

With walkman secured on my head, I wail along with Steven Tyler, discussing love in an elevator while putting away my clothes for the summer per Mother's instructions. She didn't care for boxes and suitcases scattered amidst my ghost of a room with its remnants of high school memorabilia. But I like the clutter. It gives my wall-to-wall pink room some edge.

My first box: jeans. When I reach the bottom of the stack, I find my special Def Leppards, all ripped and frayed. Oh how Joe Elliot wore these, well not these exact jeans, so pleasingly in the *Pour Some Sugar On Me* video! I begged Mom to shell out $60 for the pair, assuring her the tattered pants would be shown off on every possible occasion. I can count on one hand the number of times I've worn them.

They're a real bitch to pull on, with my toes catching on every rip as my feet struggle to reach their freedom. So 1988, these are. I don't have the heart to rid of them. Maybe it's because that first night when I wore them out a mohawked drunk approached me, wagging his painted fingernails and said, "YOU! Rockstar! In the jeans! Remember us little people." I know the guy was making fun of me, but I soaked up his words. To this day, I believe it. Maybe I won't literally be a rock star. However. I want to make my mark.

What the hell. I don't have much else to do right now. I whip off my sweat shorts and force the bitchin' jeans on.

Now I'm in character. Positioned in front of my mirror, testing out poses, with my hand as my microphone, I belt it out Aerosmith with all my heart.

"Bravo," shouts a voice from the hallway.

I swing my head in terror to match the face with the voice. Throwing off my headphones I want to shout, but I'm suddenly mute. Leaning against the door, is my ex-boyfriend Christopher. His hair has grown shoulder-length and his eyes are withdrawn, pale. His good-looks have morphed into something reminding me of a sad, little possum.

"I knocked and called out. No one answered, but I could hear you wailing." His lips curl into a smile, as if he's trying to charm me.

"You can't just walk into people's houses uninvited," I say pointing to the door. "It's called breaking and entering."

He inches inside my doorway and glances around at my boxes on the floor. "Looks like you're moving home?"

I shake my head. "God no. I am most definitely not moving home." Wondering where my parents have vanished to, I shove a box his way to create a barrier between us.

Chris drops his head, rubbing his eyes.

"How long you back for then? Was thinking we could do something together, you know?" He looks up at me, sheepishly. "Like old times?"

My stomach clenches, and I feel a scowl form on my face.

"I just mean as friends," he adds quickly. "Like get wasted or something. Shit Amy, there ain't a fuckin' song on the radio that don't make me think of you. Remember when we used to dream about starting our own rock band?"

"*Doesn't* make me think of you."

"Huh?"

"The correct way to say that would be, 'Shit Amy, there *isn't* a fucking song on the radio that *doesn't* make me think of you.' Anyway, it's been three years, Chris. Three years. I hardly ever come home, but when I do, you seem to show up. You show up more now than you did when we were dating. Do you just keep driving by the house, waiting to see my car?"

He doesn't respond.

"Please move on. Find a girlfriend who likes to drive

around and smoke dope with you."

He looks straight at me. "College made you a stuck up bitch. Your dad works in a plant here. He ain't no better than anyone."

I sigh. Then I nod. "You're right. So why would you want to be with a stuck-up bitch like me?"

I start tapping my foot. "Please go, Chris. Before I start yelling for my dad."

He begins to turn around. But before he leaves he mutters, "Nice jeans. Tell your mom hi. At least she's always nice to me."

"Mom's a politician."

Once he's gone, I consider whether I really want to unpack. The transitory nature of living out of a suitcase has a certain appeal right now.

Chris pokes his head back in.

"Maybe we should kiss one more time." He's holding on to the side of the door. "An experiment to see if you have any feelings left for me. If you don't, I'll never bug you again. If you do, we get back together."

His blood-shot eyes make it difficult for me to take him seriously.

As I step over the box, toward the door, he starts toward me, his arms outstretched. I shake my head, put my hand out, then grab the door.

"Goodbye, Chris!"

I close the door, and listen for him to leave. Then I run to the backyard to find my mother who's kneeling in a patch of dirt, planting bulbous yellow flowers,

"Guess who I just kicked out of my room?"

"It better not have been a mouse," she says while digging a hole.

"Chris."

"Good. Not a rodent."

"That's debatable," I say sitting down next to her, taking the flowers out of their plastic containers.

"The poor kid's a little lost. I hope he can find his way."

"He can find his way without stalking me."

Mom looks up. "Nice to see you wearing those pricey jeans for once." She takes a plant from my hand and begins to peel off the bound roots. "You were crazy about Chris at one time, you know. And he was your pal, long before you dated. Just because you go off to college doesn't mean you should stop caring for someone."

"Mom!" The summer has just gotten hotter. "What are you saying? He's gone all creepy! A drug addict! I know you want more for me."

I hop up to go back inside. Mom looks at me, her gloved hand covering her squinty eyes. "Amy, I'm not suggesting you get back together. Just show some compassion. You know he's had a rough life."

Not that rough. Lots of kids' parents get divorced. I swear teachers swooned over him because he had a certain Bon Jovi appeal with his looks and his awesome voice. That talent rotted away when he flunked out his freshman year at Simpson college, giving up his full-ride.

I stomp back into my room and curl into my bed, now feeling a bit nauseated.

The summer's gonna be shitty, just like I predicted.

It's really not so much about my parents anymore; I can take the criticism, I think. But when I see how Chris ruined his life and wasted his talent?

I either want to wretch or scream.

CHAPTER 5
MATERIAL GIRL

MAY 1992

I've never walked inside this bank before with its colonial brick and imposing white columns. And here I am for an interview, sporting my mother's black polyester suit from JC Penney. My bank, a few blocks away, has slightly darker red bricks and is distinguished by a parapet. No stately columns. Of course, I'm more than willing to switch banks with the offer of a job. I do like this institution's proximity to the downtown, in the historic square with all the quaint shops and the cathedral-like Courthouse and infamous Foxy Pub.

"I'm here to see Roger Slaughter," I say attempting to use a professional tone, which comes out sounding more like a breathy impression of Cher. I clear my throat.

A young receptionist faces me. I'm immediately distracted by stitches near her eyebrows, not quite hidden behind her red-framed glasses.

"Amy Gaer?"

I nod, trying to recognize the girl. "Did we go to high school together?"

"Not unless you graduated from Omaha Prep." She stands, pointing to her name tag. "Penny. Penny Popp. Pleasure." Stepping away from her desk, she pokes her head into the large office in the corner. When she returns she says, "I gave him the look. Should be out in no time."

After Penny offers me a seat in the waiting room, I find myself sitting across from a man shrouded behind a newspaper. He wears tattered work boots, stained jeans, and sounds as if he's snoring, or breathing impressively loud.

"They just keep getting better lookin' round here," says the voice peeking over the paper.

I keep my head down, studying my résumé.

The voice repeats the comment, only louder.

I look up.

Looking somewhat jaundice, he crumples his paper and waddles his way to a seat next to me, permeating my space with body odor and greasy food. I smile at him.

"Sales. I bet yer in sales," says the man.

I shake my head.

"Amy, I didn't offer you anything to drink," interrupts Penny. "What can I get you?"

My parched throat is dying for a sip of a

Diet Coke which I presume will make me especially sharp. "No thanks," I say. "I'm fine."

"You never offer me anything, Miss Penny," says the man. "What makes her sh- sh- shit not stink?"

Penny rolls her eyes, this time without moving her eyebrows. Then she points her finger directly at that man. "Gordon, I've made you two pots of coffee, and you've eaten six rolls here today. What more could you want?"

He giggles, or coughs, I'm not sure.

Under her breath she says, "And no one has made better use of the men's restroom than you."

As I take a sideward glance, Gordon is wringing his hands–almost non-stop. Perhaps he has a tic, or a compulsion disorder? Or maybe he is mentally challenged.

Feeling a wave of sympathy, I turn to Gordon, "So, what kind of rolls did you have today?"

"Gl-gl-glazed donut. Jelly-fill with sprinkles. Two cinnamon rolls." He continues to describe the types and approximate sizes of his feast with periodic bouts of stuttering. I keep focused on him, pretending to be interested, tuning out as he goes into a dissertation on how pastries affect his bowels.

A lanky man in a light gray suit emerges from the corner office to interrupt my conversation with Gordon. Caught off-guard, I'm expecting a fat, silver-haired dude in expensive threads. So I bounce up to extend my hand and have him test my knowledge of the handshake. I look him in the eye with my un-flirtatious smile, since of course, he's old and I want to evoke professionalism. I try not to focus on his sweaty palms. As I follow him into his office, Gordon wishes me luck and I offer him a wink. I hold back my laugh when Gordon attempts to wink back.

Roger begins the interview by shuffling his al-ready clean desk around and asking me about my endeavor into business, after studying English. In-stead of telling him about my *Working Girl* movie night I say, "My plan shifted away from law school when I really started to think about economics. Economics of the world. Economics of the nation. Economics of my individual situation. I took a few classes and really felt it was an important course of study for me to pursue if I wanted to make a contri-bution."

Roger seems to be smiling like a proud chef, and I'm feeling like I should be given the Oscar for my performance. We continue to visit as he explains his vision for a management trainee program and I respond to his questions with, of course, completely ingenious answers.

"While I don't have banking experience, I'm smart. A quick learner."

"Weaknesses? I'd have to say I can be pretty hard on myself. I'm somewhat of a, well, perfection-ist."

Just as we're on a roll, Penny buzzes in.

"Rog? You're next candidate is here."

What? Next candidate?

Roger looks to his watch and stands, signaling the end of the interview. I rise quickly, following his lead.

"Amy, it's been nice. We'll be calling you next week with a decision."

"Fabulous!"

Fabulous? My choice of the word fabulous keeps me from babbling any more, so I just smile. After we shake hands, I realize now both of our hands are sweaty.

Once I step out, my heart falls as I catch sight of the next applicant's back. I'm certain it's someone I know well. I attempt a quick escape. But before I have a chance to sneak away, I hear, "Hey girlie!"

It's Shandy. Shandy Wilson. My one-time best friend turned nemesis. Shandy Wilson. Despite my superior abilities as a singer and a dancer, guess who played Sandy in Grease? Shandy Wilson. I'll never, ever get over that. No matter how cool the part of Rizzo is supposed to be.

"Nice to see you, Shandy." I turn around to face our 1988 homecoming queen. There she is, with her stupid perky nose, taking a job opportunity away from me. The only consolation I feel is Shandy has gained a few pounds. Of course, the extra pounds make her boobs look particularly nice.

She hugs me as if we're dear friends.

"You're not applying for this position are you?" She asks. "Miss Law School?"

I pull away, nodding my head. "Actually, I am. Taking another semester to get my business degree. Holding off on law school. For now."

Smiling like she's in a pageant, she says, "Well, law school is pretty ambitious for someone who was gonna be a rock star. Hey! Have you seen Chris lately? You're probably planning a reunion this summer."

My snaky-eyes emerge while she continues to smile just as Roger joins us. I salute myself away, trying not to judge their interaction. But Shandy's so audacious, playing up her normal cheesy, pleasy self. She still makes me want to puke.

After leaving the bank, I whip off my jacket in the somewhat brutal sun. Feeling unnerved by the knowledge of my new competition, I decide to stroll around the square to let out some newly-acquired steam. It's vitally important for me to get this job. What can I do to make sure Shandy does not get this job? I know! I could arrange for her to get into a terrible accident so that she couldn't work for the summer! Perfect. I just need to hire a hit man. Maybe Chris can do it.

That would never work. Chris would think I want to get back together with him.

I dawdle around looking through the windows, and soon my mood evens itself out. The merchants and their summer-themed displays amuse me. Clothing stores use lawn chairs and beach towels to parade bright summer fashions. The hardware store has every piece of gardening tool arranged in eye-catching rows. The insurance agency uses umbrellas with a sign saying, "Don't get caught in the rain." Cute but ill-conceived idea. It's bad luck to have an open umbrella inside.

I pass a few older people I don't know, smiling at them. They smile back. I'm sure they're impressed by a young person in such a professional-looking suit. Admittedly, I feel mature. It's not Burberry, but it feels fancy. To think, I almost had a real job. A bank job, in my hands. It would've made the summer in Fox Plaine tolerable.

Oh Amy.

It's only three months. Three months of free laundry and food. Speaking of food. I find myself standing in front of the Kit Bakery, ogling the various confections. Dutch apple pies. Glazed donuts. Monster-sized sugar cookies decorated like daisies. Bear claws. Oh. Dutch letters whisper to me, snaking a platter in the shape of a big S. I sneak in to purchase a crispy almond flavored treat.

I start back to the parking lot, crunching off bits of the buttery flakes while the almond paste melts in my mouth. A jacket in one hand, a pastry cradled in the other. Crumbs cover my shirt and trail from my mouth. I better exit quickly before I see Shandy again in all my confectionary glory. After throwing my jacket in the car, I hop into the seat.

And gasp.

Pain pierces through my ass.

"SONUVABITCH!"

The damn safety pin. A quick jump frees the culprit, but not the pain. My seamstress abilities are limited to the use of a safety pin. I gathered the extra material in the back of Mom's skirt with the pin which was perfectly hidden under the matching jacket, but gapingly apparent without it.

Nice. I'm a mess. Ass hurting. Goo all over me. I'm almost in the real world now and I hardly have my shit together. I need some luck on my side.

Where's my three-legged pig? Why didn't I bring it today?

Nick's Journal

APRIL 18, 1987

Wedding day to Sarah. The love of my life!

I'm scribbling notes fast, on the steps of our new, old farmhouse as my wife lays sleeping in the next room.

I was nervous during the engagement. Most men are nervous about this kind of stuff, I think. But I'll never meet anyone like Sarah. We feel right together. She knows what it takes to live on a farm. She grew up on one.

I hope I made the day special for her. The day didn't start off so great with Sara all upset. I thought the photographer was going to walk out on us. Sarah's mom is such a bitch! Nitpicking at her, telling her she should've lost more weight before the wedding. Once I told Sarah she was the most beautiful woman in the world, she seemed to be fine the rest of the day.

She spent most of the reception dancing with her friends which was fine with me. I hate to dance. But she was happy. That makes me happy.

Tomorrow we're off to Vegas for three days. All I could afford. She loves to gamble and hopes to strike it rich. Ha! No matter. It's the start of a new and great life together.

CHAPTER 6
CENTERFIELD

MAY 1992

"Lyn Axland!" I toast with the clink of our beer cans. "Thanks for taking me out tonight. The baseball game was... what's the word? Stimulating!"

"You don't have to leave Loam County to have a good time," she says.

I nod, a bit sheepish, wondering if my friend is offended about my lack of correspondence. It's been since Christmas since we last talked. "How are things at the vet clinic?"

"Saving puppy lives!" she says, glancing around. "I thought the players would be in here by now. Hope they didn't ditch Perling to go back to Fox Plaine. This has been the party town all summer."

Eddie's Clubhouse apparently takes pride in being located "100 steps from the ballpark" as indicated on the kitschy wallboard posted by the entrance. Despite the lack of college students, I hardly feel depressed. I sense a spirited night to arrive any minute.

"I get why," I say, "This place certainly has charm."

The fluorescent lighting in this tavern glows with magnificence. I'm not sure how it'll play out on my reflection after a night of shots. Right now, however, it creates a bright mood. Pleasant actually. Other than the lighting, the bar has a similar Loam County ambience of dark paneling, beer signs, and college football team posters. The U of Iowa Hawkeye poster gives a pinch at my heart.

"Ready for some shots?" Lyn asks.

I glance toward the bar where a row of farmers sit, wearing a variety of seed corn hats. One lady stands behind the row of men, listening to their conversation, occasionally contributing with a raspy laugh. She looks rough, tunnels etched into her skin. I wonder why she'd tolerate standing behind them. And why they wouldn't offer her a seat.

"Just you and me?" I point to the counter of farmers. "Or should we ask them as well?"

"It might liven up the place," she says getting up after downing her beer. "Be right back."

I wander to the juke box. After searching through the mostly-country-music selection, the lady standing by the bar hollers over, "You better not be yanking my Hanky! I can't stand that heavy metal shit."

"Just browsing," I say. Then I turn back. "Do you consider ACDC heavy metal?"

But she's not listening to me anymore. Her cigarette has become her main intention, with each determined drag. I continue my search through the land of no-rock-bands when lo and behold, White-snake appears!

That's when the door flies open, streaming of baseball players, uniformed in grays and reds, be-smudged with dirt. My ears fill with the cacophony of grumbling and shouts of men, seemingly on a quest. As testosterone floods the air, I feel a tad out of place. Yet. I can't help but feel I'm just in the right place.

I ogle the entrants inconspicuously, and one particular baseball player from the gray team piques my interest. I can't place him from high school. And he would definitely be someone I'd remember. Cute only begins to describe him. Defined jawline, square chin. Chilling eyes—almost threatening. A few blondish hairs escape his cap, which he wears haphazardly as if it were about to fall off. He stands with his muscly arms crossed, assured-like as a crowd of players nest around him, offering him beer. He smiles at his pals. Ooh. That playful grin just made my heart take a turn.

As I edge my way through a crowd of players, attempting to catch glimpses of cute baseball guy, I see his eyes float over the top and through the person speaking to him right now. Did I just sense his smile transform into sadness? Or, am I imagining things? Perhaps it's the wretched country song playing on the jukebox. After a few minutes of discreet observation, he's engaged in debate. I believe I've mistaken sadness for intense baseball discussion.

Making my way back to the table, I find Lyn now surrounded by a few players including her brother.

"Luckily I found you," I say to Lyn. "Patronage was quadrupled. And some."

She points to her t-shirt. "Just look for the Budweiser sign."

Right. It's always clever to wear beer shirts to a bar.

With that thirsty look in her eye, she hands me the glass to toast. I down the liquid fire and slam the shot on the table.

Tequila.

Looking around, but not seeing what I need, I shout, "No lime or salt?"

"They were out," Lyn says passing me a beer chaser. Then she leans over to me. "What do ya think of him? The dude talking to my bro?"

I glance over to see Lyn's brother and his buddy locked in a deep conversation with each other. This boy's not interested in Lyn. Or any other *girl.* Not with that shirt tucked in, perfectly coifed hair, and his undivided attention on Lyn's brother. "He's not ugly," I whisper.

Lyn pulls herself into their conversation, not thinking herself as the intruder. After gulping half my bottle of beer, I excuse myself to the restroom–

with intentions to meander the premise.

"Hey, aren't you Amy Gaer?"

Someone near cute baseball player nudges me. He's short, stocky and reminds me of a younger version of Elmer Fudd—except his face is more kindly. I lean in to form a circle, thankful for my new position in the room. I nod and smile, trying hard not to bat my eyes.

"Clay Jensen's cousin, right?" says stocky. "Clay and I played football together when we took our team to State." He extends his hand. "Brad Smith, played center. I remember seeing you at Clay's graduation party way back when. You were probably like, in junior high back then?"

"I thought you looked familiar," I lie to Brad, as I steal more glances at cute baseball guy. Go ahead, Amy. Knock his socks off with your charming wit. "Actually, I was a freshman when Clay graduated." Think. Think. I turn to Adonis. "You look familiar. Were you at Clay's party?"

Brilliant. Simply brilliant.

He shifts in his shoes, sipping his beer. Then I think to myself, why didn't I just ask him when he graduated?

"Not sure I remember."

Am I really a college graduate? Who talks about high school graduation parties from 1985?

"I'm Nick Klein," he adds. "I work part-time for your dad at Dawson Manufacturing."

He must know me! He knows my dad!

"That's it. I must have spotted you down at the plant!"

I lie, but he seems convinced. Frankly, it would never occur to me to be on the lookout at the plant.

"Can I get you a beer?" Brad asks, checking my hands for a drink.

"Yup," Nick says finishing off his drink. "I'm ready."

Brad turns away with no small wince.

"I just came from college, where guys emphasize how they can't really afford to buy you beer."

Nick nods with a polite smile, staring past me. "Brad can afford it."

The conversation has come to a pause. Come on, Amy. Engage him! Be interesting.

"So," I say, "You know my Dad?"

"He's my boss."

He doesn't offer any more information. I'm trying to decide if he's shy, rude, or simply not interested in conversing with me. I'm willing to press just a little more.

"Working part-time?" I ask.

Nick nods slowly. His eyes catch mine. For approximately five seconds. His eyes are so dark, his pupils blend into his irises. I can hardly detect any other speck of color. I can detect, however, a hint of interest in me.

"So, do you go to school somewhere?" I attempt the conversation again.

Nick finishes his beer. "I farm."

"Really?" I say. "You don't look like a farmer."

Way too hot to be a farmer.

The comment makes him crack a smile. Then his eyes linger on me when he says, "How are farmers supposed to look?"

I shrug, just as Brad joins us with bottles of beers. Brad asks me if I'm in college. But before I have a chance to explain too much of my current student status, Brad interrupts me by explaining his enrollment at Iowa State University and his plans on becoming a coach. I'm trying to listen to Brad, but my eyes keep floating to Nick. Finally, I find a break in Brad's narrative.

"Didn't you have a home run tonight?" I ask Nick.

Instead of responding, Nick takes a drink as Brad knocks him on the shoulder. "Keep that up and you could take me out of fourth position yet." Brad continues on for several minutes about his own batting statistics. When I notice a dart board across the room, I disrupt the monologue. "Nick, do you like to play darts?"

Nick scratches his cheek, glancing at his friend. For a moment, I feel a wisp of guilt over my tact. Then Brad points to someone across the bar. "Rooney! You piece of shit." Brad steps away, mumbling about a need to catch up with another teammate.

"You really want to play darts?" Nick asks

after Brad leaves us.

"Why not?"

Nick takes a deep breath, then a drink of his beer.

"Follow me." Nick's voice is so quiet, I'm straining to hear him. But I don't mind leaning in to him. As soon as he rests his hand on the small of my back, I feel my breath hiccup. He keeps hold, directing me to the corner of the bar.

"I'm not so good at this," I admit.

"We should put some money on it then?"

"You'd be smart to."

Nick hands me three darts and invites me to do a practice throw. The dart sticks into the wall, about an inch from the board.

"Maybe I should give you a quick lesson."

Positioning himself closely behind me, Nick has the warm smell of an athlete, without the pungency. I detect a fragment of cologne, or maybe it's just something like Dial soap. No matter, I breath it in. He rests the dart in my hand, wrapping his fingers around mine, then points at the board. Straightening my elbow, he whispers, "Now close one eye and aim for the bulls-eye. You do know what the bulls-eye is?"

I glance at back at him, and a smile is born out of me. If I move much closer, I'd feel his after-five stubble. With a mild sway, I look back and try to focus toward the center of the dart board. But I'm caught up in Nick's proximity. It seems now I've completely lost my breath.

"Use your wrist and launch it straight in."

In one quick movement the dart is flying through the air. It lands near the bulls-eye.

Unfortunately for me, Nick lets go of my hand, chucks me on the shoulder and steps away. "See! You got it. Now we have a game."

I consider relapsing into my initial skill-level, so Nick can show me once again what to do. But I don't. We play three games, in which he slaughters me.

When we're finished he extends his hand for a hive-five, then changes his expression practically in mid-flight.

"Can we sit down?" he asks.

"Are you okay?"

"You should know something."

"Okay," I say, giggling from the amount of beer I've consumed. My insides are churning with this gorgeous man looking into my eyes.

"I'm married."

I choke on my laughter. He takes my hand and leads me to a small table. He lowers his head and speaks quietly. "My wife left me two weeks ago."

With my mouth agape, I wait for him to say more. Finally I offer, "I'm so sorry."

He nods, picking at his nails. "It's been over longer than two weeks. I wanted to be honest with you. And didn't want you to think I'm trying to pick you up on the rebound."

"I didn't think you were trying to pick me up at all. I approached you, remember?"

My Whitesnake is finally playing. I wonder if he detects the coincidence in the selection. *Here I Go Again.*

"I'd really like to call you," he says so quietly I almost don't hear him. Then he finally looks up at me. "But it's complicated right now."

"I'm just here for the summer anyway. If you ever feel like just hanging out or... " I hesitate to suggest anything. "Maybe I'll run into you at another baseball game."

"I'd like running into you again," he says. "And hearing you sing more."

"Huh?"

"You have a great voice."

"Have you heard me sing?"

"Every time I threw a dart. Or you threw a dart, you sang. It was good."

Never have I felt such a strong desire to go home with anyone in my life. Perhaps because I know it's not in the tarot cards tonight.

As I shrug and shake my humble head in pretend embarrassment, Lyn approaches. "Hey, good game second baseman!"

I introduce Nick to Lyn, who seems to be somewhat familiar with her since Lyn's brother is in the league.

"You had a crusher tonight," says Lyn with the cool confidence of someone who knows baseball.

"Finally," Nick says flatly. "Most of my hits have been at the warning track lately. And you know what they say about warning track power."

"Absolutely nothing," says Lyn.

"I'm lost," I admit. "Warning track power?"

"The warning track. The area just before a ball makes it over the fence," Lyn explains.

I smile at the metaphor.

"As a matter of fact," Lyn says with a yawn. "I'd say I'm at the warning track right now. You ready Amy?"

Not really.

"We play on Sunday again at 1:00," Nick says. "If you're bored."

Lyn puts her arm around me to leave. I finger wave goodbye. As he walks back to join the crowd of baseball players, he sends me with one of those puzzling smiles, making my heart do a half-flip, somersault, and cartwheel all at once.

"Very cute, you bitch," Lyn says.

"I know, right?" I say before turning to her. "Does it matter if he's married?"

Lyn's eyes grow wide before she shrugs and keeps walking. She never has been one to pass judgement. I skip to the car as I think about the possibilities for the summer.

CHAPTER 7

DIRTY LAUNDRY

MAY 1992

My heart pumps at an accelerated tempo. Imaginary butterflies swirl around me. I picture them to be humongous, and brilliantly blue. Practically cartoonish. Without a drop of coffee in me, I dance about the kitchen, then hug my mother who's perched over the counter nibbling on some toast.

"You're up unusually early today," says Mom. "And all the perk! Did you get the job?"

I squeeze her and say, "I met someone last night!"

Mom straightens up to address me. "Met someone? In Fox Plaine?"

"Can you believe it? All those boys in Iowa City and I just happen to run across this gorgeous guy within a few days of being home."

"A gorgeous guy?" Mom asks. "Who is this mystery man?"

I look over to Dad who has now taken a reprieve from his paper to listen to the conversation. "Dad knows him." I pour myself a cup of coffee before making the announcement. "Nick Klein. His name is Nick Klein."

Dad juts his lips with an overt furrow of the brow.

"Oh," Mom utters. "Nick is... is cute."

"He's married," Dad says.

"No," I say. "His wife left him."

"Two weeks ago," Dad informs me. "He's still married."

"But the marriage was a mistake. It's over."

"You learned all this last night?"

"Actually, not so much." I join my father at the table. "We really didn't go into detail about his failed marriage. I didn't want to pry." My father begins to shake his head, while my mother continues to put dishes in the dishwasher.

"Nick's an awesome athlete. He made some great plays during the game."

"What in the world would you two have in common anyway?" Dad asks.

I sip on my coffee, not liking the full-strength flavor without my dose of milk. Then I respond. "He likes to play baseball. I like to watch him play baseball."

"I don't know Nick very well," Mom says while clearing off Dad's breakfast dishes. "And I'm sure he's a super guy and all, but you might want to think about what you're getting into." She stops to rub my shoulder. "Two weeks is a short time to be separated. They've only been married a couple of years." She cocks her head, looking toward my dad. "Didn't we go to that wedding, Curt? Yes! We Did! It was beautiful! All the bridesmaids with their pastel dresses. And the flowers were absolutely gorgeous. Anyway, that's not the point. We don't want to see you get hurt."

"I think I'm old enough to make my own decisions. And I'm not stupid."

Another drawback of living at home. My every move will be monitored.

Folding his paper, Dad pulls himself up to kiss my mom goodbye. "Well you're stupid if you mess with a married man."

Dad pats my shoulder on his way out the door.

Mom pulls my chin up. "Amy, I'm glad you're home. I want you to have a good summer." She looks down for a moment then says, "But don't make it messy."

I gaze at her, wishing I could explain the connection I felt with this boy in a baseball uniform last night. And my need for a distraction this summer. If I'm gonna be pouring coffee for Shandy Wilson, I might as well have some fun.

However. Judging from the anxiety in her eyes, I'm inclined to downplay any plans of romance. "It'll probably turn out to be nothing. We only chatted at a bar."

Mom lowers my bangs which have expanded to new heights over night. "I'm sure you boosted his spirits. You have a knack for that."

She kisses my head and sets off to finish getting ready for work...at the Courthouse, the epicenter for any county gossip. She'll probably hear I'm dating a married man. It's no wonder she's concerned.

But the truth? I'm undaunted by my parents' reluctance. The butterflies continue to flutter with the image of the baseball player and his dark, bewitching eyes.

Suddenly, lunch plans occur. It's been too long since I've toured my father's plant.

CHAPTER 8
HOW WILL I KNOW?

MAY 1992

Listless. I feel so listless. Anxiety is consuming me. While I played it cool for Nick when he told me of his situation, cool really isn't my thing. I assumed he'd call. Keeping busy is my way of dealing with his apparent neglect. So far today, I've:

–Jogged through town. Toured old neighborhoods. Decided I love yellow houses of the cottage variety. Cheery.

–Performed a concert on my untuned Steinway. One lone cricket chirped in accompaniment as I paid homage to Blondie, Fleetwood Mac, and Donna Summer.

–Started a book on the Civil War. Fell asleep at the Battle of Fort Sumter. Need to expand my parents' bookshelf. No person should survive on history chronicles alone.

–Stared at the phone, commanding it to ring.

I'd take a call from just about anyone right now.

It's only ten in the morning. I'm walking around my parents' house, wistfully in thought. Maybe I should return to Iowa City. Or just visit the Fox Plaine Library.

That's when the phone awakens.

CHAPTER 9

WORKING MAN

MAY 1992

In my khaki skirt and pink-striped pullover, I step through Dawson's Manufacturing to my dad's office to share my joy. And allow him to buy me lunch. And inspect the scenery.

Oil and machinery waft through the air. As I catch the sight of the grease-splattered workers, I begin to question myself. Will I recognize Nick in this setting, in my sober state? Will he still be as Adonis-like as I remember?

I tap on Dad's door. He looks up over his computer, motioning me in.

"Amos!" Dad says, "You look nice. What brings you here?"

I put my hands on my hips to announce, "Just thought you'd like to meet Loam State Bank's newest management trainee." I can't help but hop and clap for myself.

"Good news," Dad says. "When do you start?"

"Not sure." Cupping my hands over eyes, I spy on the activity outside his window. "June maybe."

"What's the pay?"

"Not sure."

"What department you starting in?"

"Not entirely sure about that either."

"Are you sure you were offered a job?"

"Pretty sure," I say. "Meeting with Roger this afternoon to go over details. But I thought we could go to lunch to celebrate."

Dad looks at his watch. "I can manage that."

As Dad organizes his desk to leave, I notice a few gray hairs beginning to streak his hair. He's always appeared so youthful to me with his clipped mustache and lean build. It suddenly occurs to me, he's aging and I'm an adult. Soon, I'll have a career and he'll be retiring. He'll be hanging around in his sweat shorts drinking coffee while I'm buzzing around from meeting to meeting in my corporate attire. The image of me in a smart business suit is dispelled. Someone is staring at me through my father's glass door.

"Chris? Chris!" I shout. "What the–?"

"Easy Amy," says my father as he ushers me out of his office while Chris stands there gaping at me. "He works for me now."

My jaw grinds as I hold back my instinct to

start ranting at my father for hiring him.

"The mud pump's working real good now," Chris says as I feel him facing me, although my eyes are directed at the floor. "You want me to learn any of those other machines this afternoon?"

"Not yet," says my dad. "But thanks for the update."

I tap my foot. "Ready Dad?"

As soon as we step away I say "Ridiculous. Messed up. Why would you ever hire that loser?" I'm shaking my head as if I'm wagging my finger at my dad. "I can't imagine he ever gives you status reports on the mud pumps!"

"Didn't know I had to run my hiring decisions through my daughter."

My arms are tightly wrapped around my belly. I think about the scowl on my face. And consider who I might see. I take a deep breath and relax the muscles in my cheeks.

"His uncle is my best foreman. He wanted to hire Chris after he got fired from the beef plant."

"Nice," I say in a loud whisper. "How's that working out?"

My dad stops walking for a moment. Then he peers down at me before scooting off again.

We exit the plant. I find myself sorely disappointed. Besides running into my psycho ex, there was no sign of Nick anywhere. And I observed the place as if I were Sherlock Holmes himself. Nick was definitely not there.

After we buckle up, my dad sets the key in the ignition. But he stares straight ahead, still as a crouching tiger. He's pensive. I'm prepared.

"You know, Amy, I am proud of you. Smart. A double major. But there's more to the real world you know."

"I know, Dad. I've had jobs. I'll have a real job soon."

"Lots of college interns come in with their engineering degrees who wouldn't think of having a beer with Chris. Or Nick. I'd hire Nick over an engineer any day." He starts the truck. "Anyway, I don't want you walking into the bank like you know everything. Modesty goes a long way in earning respect."

"Do you really think I'd go into a place and act like I'm better than someone else? You should know me better than that."

Dad shrugs.

"You do know that Chris stalks me, don't you?"

"I don't think he means to do that," he says. "Try not being so bitchy to him."

My parents are confused a bit on the Chris issue. He cheated on me. And started doing drugs. I feel the burn of chagrin feed into my cheeks and ears.

How can my own father think of me as a snob? Like snooty Shandy Wilson?

"Dad, I hope you know I don't want to let you

down. I never want to let you or Mom down."

"Oh, Amos," says Dad. "Life's not about pleasing your parents. I thought you at least figured that one out."

I don't believe that. Not one bit.

CHAPTER 10
YOU'VE GOT A FRIEND

JUNE 1992

Feeling all polished in my my mother's smart navy jumper, I'm headed to my first day of work at the Loam County Bank. To control my anxiety, I take deep breaths just like I learned in Meditation 101. As I inhale, I wonder if I'm starting to sound like Gordon.

Glancing at myself in the rearview mirror before I climb out of my car, I can't help but wonder. How in the world did I get this position over Shandy? Maybe she was over-qualified. Or demanded more money. I wouldn't mind running into Shandy now. But somehow, I think Shandy is already headed back to her university town to find a much more glorious position than this.

I tap towards the pillared entrance to find Penny waiting to welcome me, clipboard in hand.

With a wry smile she says, "Let's take care of the most important details first. Which night are you available to go out for drinks?"

My shoulders drop as my smile settles in. "Only one night?"

She gestures for me to follow her as I notice a few friendly faces saying hello and congratulating me.

"By the way," she says as we pass through the building,"You can thank me for the job. Me and Gordon, that is."

"What do you mean?" I ask, trying to keep up in my new patent heels, which seem to have a vendetta against my toes.

"I told Roger how nice you treated our Gordon. And what a stuck-up wench that Shandy was. She actually asked me if I could do something about him." Penny glances back to me. "Can you believe that? At an interview?"

Halting before an office located centrally in the building, Penny swirls around to face me. "Ginny Berg pretty much runs this place. Besides me, obviously. She's got the teller and operations staff, and runs the consumer loans division. Consider her your formal mentor for the summer." Penny shifts on her feet. I notice her bright blue flats, matching her bright blue frames. "Anyway, a few of us like to get together at the Foxy every week. It wouldn't be the worst thing in the world to hang out with someone my age. Someone a little younger than the 'The

Mothers.'"

"The Mothers?"

Penny points to the teller line on the other side of the building. "Those women right there. You'll love them." Penny pulls down her glasses. "It's a requirement."

Penny steps back as I meet Ginny who greets me in such a zealous way I feel she's about to kiss me. Dazed by her presence, I find myself staring up at the tall, black-haired, somewhat exotic looking woman, wondering how Fox Plaine germinated such a beautiful and polished lady. Could she possibly be from here? She wears a creme-colored dress shirt with flowy black trousers – nothing akin to a stodgy bank uniform I was concerned I might encounter, or be forced to wear.

Sitting back on the corner of her desk which is nearly covered with documents, Ginny ignores pleasantries, diving right into my history. "I hear you have a diverse background. An English major, studying business? How creative. Well, there is so much I want you to learn this summer from the technical to the-not-so-technical. But I have a personal mission to get more young women empowered in business. And when Roger told me he hired you, a girl, for the trainee position, I almost did a cartwheel!" She pats her hands on her desk. "So, you ready to take on the bank?"

I smile and nod ferociously, infected with her enthusiasm. My summer is really beginning to mold into some purpose.

Ginny and I scamper throughout the building to meet everyone. As I am introduced to all the staff members, I become self-conscious of my high bangs. Apparently, the hair code for banking calls for "desperately flat." Tomorrow I'll tone my coiffure down a bit. But for now I challenge myself to memorize everyone's name, to atone for my offensive, rock-star hairdo. Most everyone has welcomed me with the typical hometown warmth I'm used to, but I catch their eyes floating up to the top of my head. I'll do whatever it takes to earn the respect of this placid crowd.

"Before I send you off to your first assignment on the teller line, I want you to meet my right hand man." Ginny takes me to an open area of the loan support staff, where one cubicle is distinguished with higher walls.

Sitting inside the cubicle of kid-photo-copia, is a woman wearing a teal green suit and a bouffant so stunning I could actually imagine a little bird nesting on top. At least someone else I the bank has tall hair.

"I know your mama well," says Donna after introductions. "We talk all the time at the courthouse. She's darn excited to have you home for the summer."

"I'm excited to be home," I say trying not to stare at Donna's hair.

"Really?" says Donna. "That ain't what she

told me! She said you were dreadin' it!"

I feel my ears simmer to pink. "I'm more excited now that I have this job."

Donna slaps her knee, cackling as if I've said something funny. "That's a hoot! Well, welcome aboard." She looks to Ginny. "She doing anything over here?"

"Eventually. You can show her the ropes." Ginny pats Donna on the shoulder.

"I definitely don't know nothing about no ropes. I just do what I'm told."

"Oh Donna, you don't give yourself enough credit."

Donna swivels directly toward me and says, "Good luck to you, Miss Gaer. I hope you have a knowledgeable summer."

Ginny drops me off with "The Mothers," and explains how Connie, Deb, and Linda will teach me the basics of tellering before Charlene trains me how to open checking accounts.

And teach me they do.

"You don't always have to show Ben your cleavage." Deb digs into Connie. "You trying to kill him off by giving him a heart attack? He's 85 years-old."

"How do you think I get my high customer service remarks?" Connie says.

"Ben's legally blind," Linda pipes in. "But if unbuttoning your shirt makes you feel better about yourself, we're all about boosting self-confidence at this bank. Especially for old shits like you."

I think "The Mothers" are a bit wicked.

At the end of the day I meet back with Ginny. My cheeks hurt from giving everyone my Miss America smile. And few racy laughs with The Mothers.

"Tomorrow you'll have more in-depth regulatory training and security training. I hope you're just as anxious once you start reading the regulations." She winks. "How about we call it a day? I've got some stuff to finish here tonight. Then two kids and a husband to get home to. A whole other job awaiting me..."

"Sounds glamorous!"

"It is. A glamorous life. You should see me in my sweats."

I'm not ready to be done visiting with Ginny. I want to ask her more about her life, but I sense she's ready for me to leave. And as I say goodbye, she settles in to do more work.

On my way out the door, Penny stops me.

"So?"

"I had a nice day."

"I figured that," she says. "When we going out?"

I look around. "When do you get off?"

She smiles. "In about five minutes."

CHAPTER 11

WHERE EVERYBODY KNOWS YOUR NAME

JUNE 1992

Only two patrons sit in the dark galley-style pub known as the Foxy as we stampede our way in. After much discussion, Penny convinced The Mothers to take me out tonight. Apparently, having drinks on any other evening than a Thursday is a political issue for my new coworkers.

Before I have a chance to order a beer, Penny brings a round of shots.

"Everyone is supposed to show up for work tomorrow, right?" I ask.

"A slippery nipple never got anyone in trouble."

"Oh yeah?" shouts Connie. "How many slippery nipples landed you those stitches?"

"That was tequila. And a mad boyfriend."

I steady my gaze, holding on to my shot glass. "Mad boyfriend?"

"Not what it sounds like," Penny explains, then tips back her shot, motioning for everyone else to do the same. "So I move from Omaha, to this small town to be near my boyfriend, Jeff. I gave up a pretty good job at Union Pacific, thinking the reason he won't marry me is because I live in Omaha. Anyway, I like this job okay, but seriously, I'm just saying. I took a hefty-freaking pay cut." She points to the ladies around here. "These girls all know. Anyway, I was getting all itchy one night, thumbing through a bridal magazine. I showed Jeff a picture. He told me I needed to layoff. LAY OFF! I walked right out of the house to the Foxy and got all fucked up on tequila. I was so drunk I had to walk home. Couldn't walk so well. I sort of tripped home. Hit my head on some concrete." She shrugs and sips on her beer. "Needed just a few stitches."

At first I am quiet, watching Penny as her sips transform into gulps. When her eyes meet mine, my lips crack. I'm done for. Laughter explodes. Soon the table is quaking.

"What an asshole!" I say.

After a few more beers, The Mothers question me on my love life. I have no intention of confessing anything to my new coworkers.

"My love life is getting dusty on the shelf, which is just fine right now."

"Didn't you date Chris Fekes in high school?"

asks Charlene.

My back tenses, which Deb seems to pick up on. "High school!" she says. "This girl's a college graduate. Chris barely made it out of high school. I can say that. He's my cousin's son."

"We need to find someone for this college cutie pie then," says Linda. "There's gotta be someone around here."

I begin to shake my head.

"Absoutely! Lots of fine, young men in this county. Smart ones too."

"I really don't want to be set up."

"Sure you do," says Penny.

Then my new coworkers begin to discuss a number of names. Some I recognize. Like Brad Smith "who happens to be back this summer before finishing off his Masters, or something like that." According to Linda, this nephew of her best friend, would be quite the catch since he "...was one of the football stars who took the team to State..." Evidently, I targeted the wrong baseball player at the bar. He probably would've called me by now. But talk of possibilities for me fades the moment I notice a handwritten sign posted in the back of the bar. My heart patters as the black, block letters call to me: BRAND NEW! KARAOKE!

Without speaking, I point to the machine.

None of them quit discussing my "man" situation. So I stand up to say, "Have any of you tried out that?"

No one responds.

I find the list of songs and distribute to each of my new friends, insisting that everyone choose at least one.

They resist. Initially.

"I'll go first," I say. "To ease your anxiety."

My gentle nudge is all it takes.

The first song, as usual for me, is Madonna's *Borderline* which I nail–hardly needing the machine to feed me the lyrics. The two other patrons have moved their chairs, so now we have a captive audience.

It takes only a few more shots to keep prodding the ladies on the stage. Eventually, me and my bank ladies just monopolize the stage. Journey. Tina Turner. By the time *Girls Just Want to Have Fun* is queued up, everyone's voice is squeakily primed.

As we all belt out Cyndi Lauper, I turn to see three familiar faces enter the pub. My vocals quickly fade away as I step off the stage to end my performance. How can I sing, with my curiosity piqued as Shandy, Chris, and Lyn cozy up together in a booth.

Is Shandy attempting to lead some strange campaign against me? When do these high school rivalries die?

CHAPTER 12
MOTHER

JUNE 1992

I'm sitting on the steps of our deck absorbing the end-of-day sun, *House of Mirth* on my lap, attempting to erase the memory of last night. But the scene just keeps imposing into these sentences I'm trying to read.

I had to say hi to them. If Lyn wouldn't have been with those two, I could've probably ignored them. Maybe. Who am I kidding? I totally wanted to rub it in to Shandy. But how was I supposed to know Penny was on my heels, ready to provoke Shandy?

"Drinking buddies? So that's how you got the job," Shandy said. In that way of hers that makes me want to yank sections upon sections of her blonde hair out. Honestly? I can't help but feel just a teensy bit of satisfaction thinking about Penny getting right in Shandy's face, telling her how it pays to network with the right people.

Penny paid for her bravado. Poor Penny. Stitches in the eye. Now a volcanic lump on the back of her head after the Shandy push. The bitch didn't even apologize. Just said she was glad she didn't get the job. Lyn looked like she was about to vomit from the confrontation. I could tell even Chris felt bad. But I was none too pleased when Chris grabbed my arm to say, "Looks like you will be around for the summer then."

Stop replaying. Read.

Why must a girl pay so dearly for her least escape from routine?

Every single sentence is making my mind go adrift. Now I'm thinking about the answering machine. The blazed machine which mocks me with its steady, gleaming light. Maybe the thing doesn't work right. Could Nick possibly have been an apparition? I have to belief the chance meeting meant something, despite his lack of contact. Perhaps Lyn and I are due for another baseball outing. Ugh. I seem desperate. I hate desperate.

I close the book and look above at the trees, twisting and waving at me. Large, leafy maples. Deciduous trees. De-cid-u-ous. What a pleasurable word to pronounce. De-cid-u-ous. I say it out loud. I repeat it. Birds chirp obtrusively as I sit at my lookout, *almost* making me forget the particular hope that keeps rising in me.

"How was your day?"

I scramble up to face my mother. "Busy. Mark me up as a working girl now." I want to ask her what's for supper and if she'll do some laundry for me, but I pause to consider my request. She could be tired, although she still looks amazingly perky with her trim figure, impeccable haircut, and her piercing Danish-blue eyes. She's no frump. God knows, it'll kill her the day her looks begin to fade.

"Mom?" I ask. "How do you do it all? The career, keeping up the house? Always so on top of everything."

She takes a deep breath, staring over the yard. "I smoked for a number of years. That helped."

"So I should take up smoking?"

"I think not," she says wrapping her arm around me. "Tough habit to quit."

We gaze over the town and its foliage, enjoying the breeze and the birds.

Mom smoked to escape. I've never thought about my mother ever having a plight, except her quest to find skin products to stay beautiful. Maybe she wanted more out of her life.

A brown squirrel runs across the yard.

"Mitzi would've been all over that squirrel," Mom mutters.

Cringing at the image, I bid my mother farewell. "Time for my jog." But Mom stops me.

"Amy?"

"Yes?" I'm ready for something sage, beyond smoking.

"Organization. I've always tried to be really organized. Frankly, if you want to accomplish anything, you gotta count on yourself to get things done."

Now I'm wondering if Mom feels shortchanged about the amount of support she got from Dad, or me at home. Especially since she's the county treasurer – a fairly substantive job in our region.

"One more thing," she adds. "I always check myself in the mirror. Every day. Front and back."

I nod. "Noted."

"Because you're wearing my dress backwards."

"Backwards?" I look down "It's backwards?"

"Pocket's on the right side of your back. The slit's in front."

No one has said a word to me all day. Not even my outspoken friend Penny. Mom and I stare at each other for a moment. I'm thinking she's really going to lecture me on this one. Then she bursts into laughter. She gives me a hug and asks, "Have they asked you to come back?"

"Probably taking bets on what I'm gonna wear tomorrow."

"You mean 'how' you're gonna wear it. I wouldn't worry much about it. Small town bank. Pretty forgiving. Good learning experience until you step into the big time. Wherever that may be." Mom wraps her arms around me again, and I take in her flowery perfume. For living around here, she's managed to make something with her life. And career. I wonder. Will I be able to do what she has done? Do I want to? A vision of Nick sneaks up and a glimpse of my future flashes before me.

Then the phone rings.

CHAPTER 13

PARTY TOWN

JUNE 1992

The couch makes my skin plead for cover. When grimy tweed hosts a plethora of beer spills, it tends to lose its luster.

"You sure you're okay out here?" asks Brian.

I nod, attempting to pull a thinning sheet around me.

Jean opted to lodge at Vickie's apartment. She playing a bit distant to me. Perhaps it has to do with my tempered reaction to her call. Who'd a thought I'd react so nonchalant to her invitation to Jon and Vicki's party? After all, I have been waiting for an excuse to buzz to Iowa City and see my college pals. I couldn't miss Jean's last weekend before Europe. Not even for a boy who won't call me.

"Your hometown friend seemed to have a good time," says Brian while offering me another flat pillow.

"Apparently. If passing out is the ultimate in-dicator of a good time." I look toward the bedroom door. "She barely wanted to come with me to Iowa City."

"Strange."

"He better not be trying anything in there with her."

"Well. You know Mitch," says Brian.

I know Mitch.

"Pleasant dreams, Amy. Help yourself to our empty cupboards." Brian takes his glass of chocolate milk and pads away into his room, leaving me to my thoughts. Of Mitch. And Lyn. Lyn and Mitch. Making out during Kriss Kross' *Jump* in the middle of the dance floor. "They seem to have chemistry," Brian whispered to me as we witnessed the scene. My heart flipped just a little. I lay down, eyes unable to close, still regurgitating the evening. Could I pos-sibly be jealous?

I jolt up to browse their barren bookshelf. *East of Eden* catches my attention. Wrapping my arms around the book, I collapse on the floor next to the couch. As I flip to the first page, a bedroom door creaks open. Mitch tiptoes out and crashes beside me with an unwavering smile, planted deeply on his face.

"You better not be telling me you got lucky."

He shakes his head. "Not yet." Then he pulls the book from my fingers. "Heard you walking around."

I take the book back. "Didn't know you were a Steinbeck fan."

"It's Brian's. He's well-read. Is it good?"

"English majors don't readily classify books as good or bad–"

"Must suck then."

"The book is great. Dumb-ass."

Mitch is still grinning, staring straight ahead.

"Lyn's pretty cute," he says. "Why didn't you bring her around sooner?"

I shrug. "You sure didn't waste any time getting to know her."

"Amy Shawn Gaer," Mitch pulls his face to his. "Are you jealous?"

"You're delusional."

"I spent the last four years chasing you, only to be denied at least 747 times. And suddenly! Possession strikes you! It's like, so fucking amusing."

Am I jealous of Lyn being with Mitch? Or just them as a couple? Digging my head into Mitch's chest I blubber, "I met someone back home."

"Oh," he says, patting my hair.

I lift my head to look Mitch in the eyes. "He's a farmer. And he's married."

"Now I see," Mitch nods, caressing my head. "But not really."

"I don't even see." I sit up. "Go to sleep. Treat my friend right though. Don't forget to call her." I point to his chest. "And you know what? You guys could be great together. Really great together."

Mitch kisses my cheek. "You might be getting a little ahead of yourself." He pushes himself up, taking a few steps toward his room. "But thanks for bringing her. She's kind of fun."

I throw a pillow at him as he walks away.

Fate? Luck? Superstition? Everything feels off-kilter for me right now. Maybe I need something different than a three-legged pig. I haven't picked up many pennies lately, but I haven't really been searching the ground either.

Maybe because my head has been in the clouds.

CHAPTER 14

REMEDY

JUNE 1992

"How's Jean?" asks my mother as she stands over the sink, cutting up cucumbers either for a salad or for an eye mask. "I bet she's great. Does she look fantastic, as usual, with that gorgeous head of hair?"

"She's excited," I say, although I hardly spoke to Jean after she met up with another student who had just studied in Europe. "Mitch and Lyn really hit it off."

"That's nice," says Mom after drying off her hands on a dish towel. Sitting down at the table, she puts her hand on her chin as if she wants to hear the details.

"Yeah. It's great, really," I say. "I actually had some fun giving her a makeover before the party. Got rid of the beer-themed tees in favor a denim mini-skirt. I'd say she gave Cindy Crawford a run for her money."

"So, does Jean begin her new, important job when she gets back from Europe then?"

"Yep." I say, crunching into a cucumber bite. "I met some guys named Joe. Two guys actually, named Joe. Engineering friends of Brian's."

"Oh?" Mom says with the vaguest of interest. "And you're interested I suppose? Still chasing boys like a young school girl."

I cock my head at Mom. "I wouldn't say that. But I convinced them to videotape me."

"Singing, I suppose."

"VJing, actually."

Mom nods.

"A documentary, detailing the best videos of all time," I say. "Sort of."

The Joe's got bored with me after the tequila shots and I began to pontificate about videos objectification of women. That tequila seemed to bring out the feminist in me.

"Sounds like you had a fun weekend. At least," Mom says with a detectable sigh, tapping her fingers. I'm unsure what she expects from me. Did she want me to enroll in law school? Find a mate? Become as beautiful as Jean? As she taps, I think I hear her chair squeaking. Then I realize, it's no chair squeak. I hear a yelp, from the basement.

"You did it!"

Even my mother can not hold back a grin.

Zipping downstairs, I throw the door open to the sight of a barrel-chested, tail-thwacking, wiry-haired dog. I kneel down to face his black-rimmed hazel eyes.

"Look at those eyes!" I say to the pup. "Who did your make-up, dude? You look like Iggy Pop!"

He plunks his five-inch tongue across my cheek, which draws out my laughter.

"Dad thought you could use some cheer," Mom says with a happiness I don't hear often. Dad thought *she* could use some cheer. And that's okay.

"I'm having trouble deciphering. What type of dog is he?"

"Something like a terrier."

"Is he missing some teeth?" I ask.

"The Humane Society was thrilled when we picked him. He's been there for awhile."

"His name?"

Mom sits down next to me, a selfish attempt to steal him away. "We left that up to you."

"Woolf. Two o's. After Virginia." I pull him to my lap, despite his stocky stance. "You're my little Woolfie."

"He sort of looks like a wolf," Mom says. "I guess."

"He's a descendent of the great wolf. Obviously."

As we sit and squirm around with our new pet, Mom stands up and says, "Oh Amy? There's one other noteworthy event that occurred this weekend."

I brace myself for something awful. They bought the dog to lessen the blow. My intuition is kicking in.

"Nick Klein stopped by."

I pull the puppy into my chest.

"He said he just wanted to see some of your father's old motorcycles. But I'm thinking he had an ulterior motive."

I kiss the dog on the head then sprint upstairs to find the phonebook. Once I locate the yellow brick of information, I hide out in my room, phone intact. Flipping to the listing, I find: Nick and Sarah Klein.

Unfazed.

I pick up the phone.

I put it down.

No. I'll wait. Be patient.

He stopped by. He's still thinking about me.

CHAPTER 14

CALL ME

JUNE 1992

With half of a pickle-loaf sandwich shoved down my throat, I'm plugging through another chapter of *House of Mirth* on my lunch break. It's really not a happy book at all.

Dad sets his paper aside and asks me, "How's banking? You like it?"

"Learning to become a first-rate teller has it's challenges."

"Maybe you'll figure it out after you get your finance degree."

"Hope so." I expound upon the finer points of balancing a drawer. Sometimes it takes a highly-trained team of specialists (The Mothers) to find my errors. As I'm illustrating my fascinating insights to Dad, he looks up from the newspaper and says, "Banking really is boring, isn't it?"

"The world needs bankers, Dad. Not everyone can build feeding mills."

Dad holds up his newspaper, asking, "How about quick round of the dead game?"

"Alright." I succumb to my father's morbid request, putting my book aside for now.

He announces names like Mary Wilson and Emory Beals, and I guess ages like 74 or 92. I've been wrong on every name he's pitched.

"You're really off today," Dad says.

"Lots on my mind."

There really are no winners in the dead game anyway.

As I begin to lead my antsy Woolfie outside, the phone rings. Expecting to take another message for my mother about some club or some meeting, the voice on the line makes me stumble over my feet.

"Amy?"

"Yes?" I manage to say.

"Remember me? From the baseball game?" After a pause he adds, "Nick Klein. Sorry, I guess I should tell you my name."

"Sure, Nick. I remember," I say as poised as a flight attendant, despite the butterflies swirling. "How are you?"

I've been waiting and waiting and waiting for you to call.

"Hope you're not too busy right now?"

Should I mention my father and I were just play-

ing the dead game as we scarf down some pickle-loaf?

"Not busy at all."

My dog is hopping around me, so I bend down to pet his ears with the hopes he won't pee. I'm gesturing at Dad to take the dog. But my Dad just peers at me, listening to the conversation.

No one speaks over the phone. There's only silence.

"Are you there?" I ask.

"Yeah. Uh, I was wondering if maybe you'd like to catch a movie or go out to eat. Maybe tonight if you weren't busy."

"I'd love to..." I say and continue to babble about eating places and the movies showing while my dog is jumping and crawling all over me. Finally, I hang up the phone and twirl. I don't even care that Woolfie has peed on my mother's wood floor.

"I have a date!"

Dad leers at me.

"It'll be fine," I assure him. "It's nothing serious. I would never date a married man."

"But that's exactly what you're doing."

"That's not how I see it," I say walking over and giving my Dad a hug from behind. "She left him. And Nick works for you. Isn't he a good guy? You pretty much said so yourself." I kiss Dad on the head.

"I should plan my outfit for tonight."

Bouncing upstairs, I sing out a medley of every love song that hits my brain. Then I rummage through my boxes and suitcases. This system of not using drawers isn't so bad. As I dig around in my shirts I stumble across a hard little object. When I pull it out, I can't help but smile at one of my three-legged pigs.

Maybe I do have the right number of super-stitious artifacts, after all. Good fortune is really be-fallen me!

CHAPTER 15

FIRST DATE

JUNE 1992

Four times. I've changed four times now. The only pieces of wardrobe I haven't changed are my bra and undies. But neuroses kicks in. Once I finally opt for my pink tank, my green undies seems a travesty. I change my panties.

Now. Decide. Mini-skirt or white bermudas. Do I want to appear promiscuous? Or touristy?

Mom peeks around the corner, giving me an up and down glance. "He's here."

Without any further analysis, I slip on the shorts.

After a quick check of my hair, and another quick shot of spray to keep my bangs from moving, I rush downstairs to the main entrance. But he's gone.

"Dad has confiscated him," Mom says as she

attempts to tuck in my tank shirt. "Check the shed."

I step outside on our deck, through our path of flowers to the back shed. The large door is wide open and Nick's back is turned away from me. Seeing him in person jars me–as he's merely been a fantasy in my mind for the past couple of weeks now. His sandy-blonde hair lays unencumbered from a baseball cap, tousled with a beach-like essence. I'm relieved to see him in his muscular-build, handsomely occupying a neon striped tee and khaki shorts. My mind has a tendency to embellish, and I wondered if I had made Nick into something he wasn't. Good Amy.

Dad will keep Nick here for hours, showing off his latest 1942 Indian motorcycle project. Especially with Nick asking remedial questions like the difference between Indians and Harleys.

"Hi."

He looks askance at me. "Amazing collection here."

"I know."

"You ride?"

"Not very often."

"She can drive," interrupts Dad. "But she never does anymore."

"You ready to go?" I ask, stepping in front of my dad.

"He just got here," Dad replies. "He's hardly seen any of my motorcycles yet."

"Bye, Father." I pull Nick away from the

motorcycles, and as we round the corner I spot a rusty Ford truck in the driveway. He begins to apologize for the shabby vehicle.

"I like it," I say before he says too much. "Looks like a classic to me."

He rolls his eyes as he opens the door for me, helping me in. Then he asks, "Are you always full of shit like that?"

"Sometimes."

He takes me to the Victoria Station: one of the finer steakhouses in town. Seated in a corner, we are surrounded by dark rail wood and train portraits on the wall. Most of the people around us are older, as we have chosen to eat at an early hour. Our waitress wears a Disney t-shirt and calls Nick by name.

Nick folds his menu, sliding it across the table. "I don't even need to read this."

"My mouth is watering," I say as I smell the wood-smoked meat wafting throughout the restaurant.

I comb through the menu. What to order. What to order. Steak, steak, or steak. I exaggerate. Beyond the cuts of prime rib and filet mignon, there's the fried chicken or the fried catfish. My girth should take cover.

The waitress arrives with our drinks asking for our order.

My eyes dart between my choices. I must decide. The waitress is staring at me, waiting. "Go ahead, Nick. Please."

While I search for an option with less than two-thousand calories.

"12-ounce prime rib. Hash browns with cheese. No onion. Ranch on my salad."

I scratch my head. "How about the filet? No...the catfish. I don't suppose you can broil that? No? That's fine. French fries are fine. Actually, better change that to a baked potato. No sour cream. Butter on the side. What's your soup?"

"No soup in the summer."

"What dressings do you have?"

"Just about anything."

"Poppyseed?"

"Except that."

"Ranch is fine. I'm not picky."

Once the waitress leaves, Nick asks, "That seemed tough on you."

"I can be indecisive," I say, which is not a lie. "There's a reason I'm going back to school for another semester."

"What do you want to do again? Did you tell me this?" He asks. "Is there a particular type of job you want?"

I bite my lip, imagining my future self, toiling up the corporate ladder in a sleek suit. "I want to be super successful. I know that for sure." Then, I take a bite of the bread the waitress laid on the table. It's hard, and I find myself crunching on it, chewing it much longer than is usual for a piece of bread. "At one time, I thought maybe I could become a rock star. I tried out for about a million bands in college."

"You're working at the bank right now I hear," he says as the waitress serves us our salads. "Chris Fekes told me that."

I wrinkle my nose. Do he and Chris talk? Are they friends? What has Chris told him about me?

"Do you like working at the bank?"

"I...think I do," I say, still distracted.

"You sound uncertain."

"So how well do you know Chris Fekes?" I finally ask.

Nick smiles. "I know that he's still pretty fond of you."

I groan, dropping my head back. "I'm sorry if you have to listen to anything about me."

"I don't mind," he says. "I find it completely amusing as I train him on machines."

Stabbing lettuce pieces, I decide to switch topics. "So, how about you? Why do you choose to work at Dawson's? Don't you like farming?"

"I love farming. Dawson's just gives me some extra cash right now. It takes a lot to start an operation." Nick burrows his head down, diving into his salad. Under his breath he says, "I didn't really ponder too many other options."

"I bet farming is a nice life."

He nods "Tis."

"I think when I start interviewing, I'll figure out the right job."

"Hope it's not like ordering your food!"

With an exaggerated sigh, I put my fork down. "Don't you ever worry about making the wrong choice?"

Nick slides his bowl away, then takes a drink. Oh. Gheesh. I just realize the insensitivity of my comment.

"I mean like when you go shopping for jeans or picking out a video rental..." I say in a lame attempt to recover. But Nick stares beyond me, into the next dining room. As his face turns ashen, I'm feeling stupidly embarrassed.

"I'm sorry. That was dumb to say. You okay?"

Nick continues his deadpan gaze. Then I notice his eyes following someone approaching our table.

"Shit," he mouths.

I look up to see a pretty blonde standing at our table. I should know her.

"Nick," says the girl who turns to me without smiling. "Who's your friend?"

Without looking at her or me, he says, "Amy. Amy Gaer. Curt's daughter." Nick gestures to the girl hovering over the table. "Amy, meet Sarah."

"Sarah Klein," she clarifies. "Nick's wife." Sarah leans over Nick, arms folded. "I have the divorce papers out in the car. Would you like to sign them now?" She looks at me. "With her as our witness?"

She unfolds her arms and clasps her hands

behind her back. Then she flips her hair back, and widens her stance – as if she's about to initiate a lecture.

Sarah Klein. I feel nauseated. I realize how I recognize her. She was Sarah Fletcher. Star basketball player. Everyone knew Sarah.

Nick stares straight ahead, his jaws tightly clenched. I quickly excuse myself to the restroom. I hear Sarah's voice begin to scold as I shut the door.

I splash water on my reddened face and look up in the mirror to think. As I study my features in the mirror, I notice a small crack in the lower left-hand of the mirror. A crack. A cracked mirror on our first date. My lips begin to quiver.

After waiting five minutes, in which little old ladies weave their way in and out of the restroom, I force myself to go back to our table. When I return, no one is there. My stomach lurches. I see the same little old ladies, now with sympathetic smiles, watch as I try to resist tears. Not working.

As I spin for the door, thinking I'll walk home, Nick grabs my shoulders, sitting me down.

"I am so, so sorry," he says. "You're upset?"

Of course I am, but I shake my head, hoping my tears won't leak out.

"I heard she was spending time in Omaha, so I figured Fox Plaine would be safe." He looks around, then lowers his head. "She left with her family, but if you want to leave, I understand."

Part of me says go. But then I lock into Nick's

eyes as he waits for my response. The guy's defeated. He just lost every game in the season.

"Our food is ordered," I say. "We might as well eat."

Nick nods. "Might as well."

Our conversation is sparse throughout the rest of our dinner. Nick is disengaged, but he attempts conversation – asking me about classes I'm taking this fall. He asks me the same questions a couple of times.

After the meal, he drives me home without any mention of seeing a movie.

"Maybe we can do this again sometime?" he says as he pulls into the driveway. The clock on his dashboard reads 8:07. "Under better circumstances."

I don't respond initially.

"Maybe," I say. "Thanks for dinner." Unsure what to do next, I give him a peck on the cheek. Then I scoot myself out. He rushes out to get my door, but I'm already standing outside of his truck.

He grabs my hand. "Thank *you* for the night. I really am sorry about what happened. But I promise it won't happen again. Can I call you again? When the time is better?"

I'm suddenly gun shy. Initially the wife thing didn't bother me. Seeing her in person definitely rattled me. But right now, this spectacular-looking man is staring at me, luring me into his essence with his dark, chocolate eyes. I nod and tell him yes. And wonder about the cracked mirror.

Nick's Journal

September 18, 1984

Dad opened the acceptance letter from ISU. He always told me it's rude to open other people's mail, but he opened the letter addressed to me anyway.

Mom and Dad wanted an explanation. I told them the guidance counselor said I should apply. My ACT scores were pretty good. 27. I am not a great student. Probably dumb luck my scores were that good.

Dad kept asking if I wanted to farm. I had to tell him a million times, yes. He doesn't see the need to go to college then. And I don't either really. Still, I always wonder if I'm doing the right thing.

Mom came into my room while I tossed balls in the dark. She's not convinced I'm happy with my choice. She bugged and bugged me to tell her what my second choice would be after farming. I told her if anything I might like architecture. But farming is probably for me. I know that.

And how could I do anything else with all that has happened? It would be selfish.

There isn't anything about farming I don't like. Machinery. Planting. Harvesting. Raising cattle. Mostly. I got ideas on marketing. I'm too independent to think about any other kind of life. The idea of exploring something else might be interesting. But not enough to let a good thing go.

CHAPTER 16
BUTTERFLY

JUNE 1992

"When do I get my prize?" Dad asks me as I lay in bed this Sunday morning of Father's Day.

I sit up, to first wipe the crud glued in my eyes. "Dad?" I lecture. "Did you forget something a bit more important? Like perhaps the 22nd anniversary of the birth of your only daughter?"

"Oh," he replies, as if what I've just said is of little consequence. He stands at the door and motions for me to follow him. "Hurry up. It's after six already."

Six in the morning. On a Sunday. My parents don't even attend church.

I suspect gifts await me. So I bound out of bed and race to the kitchen to find three gifts on the table. My parents splurged.

"Since we haven't bought you a college gift..."

Mom explains.

I rip open the largest package first to find a desperately-needed dual CD/ tape cassette boom box along with a Nirvana's *Nevermind* CD.

Speechless. Joy. Can't wipe the grin off my face. I have a box of CDs with nothing to play them on. Jean had the CD player in college.

"Nirvana? How progressive of you," I comment.

"They're my favorite group," Dad says wryly.

"The kid at the music store convinced us to buy the CD," Mom explains. "He said they're the next big thing."

"Could be," I say, barely paying attention to the CD, trying to get my new piece of equipment out of the box. "My opinion though? It's Pearl Jam. The group's not just a catchy name."

"We're not doing any music critiquing now." Dad moves the boom box aside. "Let's get these other gifts opened."

The second gift: two dress shirts and two skirts.

"Career apparel!" Mom says with a gleam in her eye.

Gazing at the clothing, my chest tightens. I love clothes. But suddenly the idea of building a wardrobe that cater to my job fills me with an unexpected anxiety. Isn't this what I'm working toward? I should be excited. I look up at my mother to see her pleased, proud expression. There's nothing I can do at this moment but respond with appreciation.

"Thanks a million! I doubt I'll even need safety pins."

As I open my last gift, pleasure seeps through me as I catch a glimpse of the name of one of my literary heros: Jane Austen. Before me is a box set of her novels: *Pride and Prejudice*, *Sense and Sensibility*, and *Emma*. Even better than building my wardrobe, I now have some books to build my library.

"I know you've been disenchanted with our bookshelf," Mom mentions.

"You can never go wrong with Jane Austen."

"Is it time for my prizes now?" Dad asks impatiently.

"Dad, you know how you always say the best things in life are free?"

"I never said that. I would never say that," Dad says, partially in jest.

I fetch the cake from hell, explaining how I was inspired from a cookbook I found in the library. But some proclivity for baking is definitely required. And despite being born and raised in the baking capital of the world, I can't say I have any sort of talent for it.

"Please appreciate the fact that I began the project at 1:00 yesterday afternoon, made three trips to the grocery store for ingredients and completed the project at 4:23 p.m. There are approximately seven layers of frosting on the cake. I had to improvise with a few things.

"What is it?" Dad asks. "Wait. Let me guess. It's a pizza. A taco pizza."

"It's a cake. Made to look like a hamburger!"

"Oh honey," Mom gushes. "That's simply adorable. Let me grab the camera."

"No Mom, you don't need to."

Mom grabs the camera and steadies her shot.

"There's even pickles on it!"

"That's supposed to be a tomato," I clarify. "The color's off."

"Of course it's a tomato. What a nice touch."

The three of us study my creation for a few moments. I break the silence, "I'm not sure we should eat it."

"No shit," Dad says. "Maybe you should teach that girl to bake."

"There are many more important things to life than baking," my mother barks.

"I'll be right back," I add. "With another gift."

"Good."

I run to my room to retrieve gifts hidden underneath my bed.

Mom instructs him to open the soft package first, which is a never-ending bundle of socks. Dad quickly opens and tosses aside. "What else?"

His next gift is a small radio for his garage. He is slightly more impressed.

"I can listen to Nirvana on this."

"I think you'll like this next one, Dad."

"I hope so," he responds with a straight face. He carefully unwraps the package to find a grainy photo of his dad (my grandfather), wearing a newsboy cap, sitting on an old motorcycle. The local photographer restored, matted, and framed the picture.

"Where did you find this?" Dad squints at the the picture, hardly moving a muscle. "My dad on a '31 VC Harley. I remember that motorcycle."

"Amy and I were going through some old pictures. We thought you'd like it." Mom comes over to my father and puts her arms around him.

"I do. I really do." Dad holds up the frame, as if to bring more light on it. "Dad would've been about 42 in this picture. Just before he died."

My tall, handsome grandfather has always been mythic to me. Apparently, he was an ingenious mechanic, like my father, who died in a trucking accident in one of those Midwestern blizzard storms.

"Did you look all through the wrapping?" I ask. "There's more."

He pulls out a three-page essay I wrote in college called *Grandpa.* "I don't think I ever shared it with you. The assignment was to write about someone you didn't know, but who influenced your life in some way."

I watch my dad read it, and wonder what's circling behind the intensity of his forehead. Have I messed up the facts? Or have I not depicted my grandfather accurately, based on my version of family lore?

When he's finished, he puts the papers down and stares straight ahead. "Dad woulda loved reading this about himself."

"Did you like it?"

Dad nods, with as much of a smile as he is capable.

"Because I actually wrote a song about him the other day. Well... it's about you and your dad." I pull my father's arm and lead him to the piano. "One more gift if you can stand it."

With my parents standing behind me, I sit on my bench and begin with my favorite chord – everyone's favorite chord. G major. My fingers progress to a simple fourth and seventh, before homing back to my G. Then I sing.

The genius of my grandpa flows to my dad
in the mechanics of his inventions
And steadiness of his hands.
The genius of my grandpa flows to me
Even though he's gone now
I'll always have his story...

After my final note, my dad pats me on the head, while clearing his throat. Mom does her mini-clap.

"Amos," he says. "Seems like your voice has gotten better since high school." He glances at my mother. "Sometimes don't you wonder if she should've pursued music with all that talent?"

"Our girl has a lot of talents. Singing will always be a nice hobby for her." Folding her hands together, Mom changes the topic. "Well! What's the plan for the rest of the day?"

"The Antique Walk is going on this weekend," Dad says, now pulling me from the piano bench.

"God no," I say, head dropping. I was hoping to skip the tradition on my birthday.

"It's Father's Day."

I could sit here, listen to my new Nirvana CD, trying not to think about Nick. Or, I could delve into *Pride and Prejudice* for the sixteenth time, trying not to think about Nick.

"You win. Antique Walk it is."

We've made it to our fifth musty shop. My parents are reveling in the old crap.

I bumble along the cramped, stifling quarters, smiling at the merchants who appear kindly and fossilized—as if they've lived here for a million years. Then something actually grabs my attention. Under a portion of the murky glass counter is a cache of antique jewelry. I scan an assortment of rings, pendants, and bracelets. My eyes fix on the butterfly broaches. Mosaic-patterns of blue, green, orange. The pieces enchant me; even though the jewelry looks like something that should be worn only by grandmas.

I have no business making any frivolous purchases, so I pick the smallest butterfly of the bunch.

As the lady wraps up my purchase she says,

"Wear this butterfly. You can bet you're gonna experience some big changes in your life."

"Really?" I say. "Well, I'm at that age.

She smiles at me and I continue to glance around while she takes a painstakingly long time to wrap my butterfly. A print by her register draws my eye–an impressionistic image of a woman reading under a tree.

"Is that Monet?" I ask.

The lady picks up the print and looks on the back. "Yep. Called *Springtime*. Not worth nothing. Just a cheap reprint. You can have it for ten bucks, if you want."

I swallow. Ten bucks is still a lot of money for me. But I agree to her tough negotiation.

A butterfly broach. A picture of a lady reading under a tree. Could this stuff from the past be clues about my future? Not sure, but I'm ready to go home with my new old stuff and listen to Nirvana.

CHAPTER 17
THE REAL WORLD

JUNE 1992

Broody. I'm broody. I hate feeling broody before I go to work. If I would've just gotten some clarification to that "timing" issue with Nick. Because I find myself, once again, in the position of lovestruck sap. Doing stupid things.

The the radio messes with my head, while I skip over any snippet of a romantic song (Def Leppard's *Hysteria*, Firehouse's *Love of a Lifetime)*. Those songs are crap to me now! Here we go. Pearl Jam. *Evenflow*. What are they saying? Something about butterflies?

I look to the butterfly pin on my dress and coach myself out of broody. Even though Eddie Vedder's singing about a homeless guy, this guitar riff is beginning to dispel my romantic notions. However. I'm anxious about walking into the bank today. And it has nothing to do with my transition into the loan department. It has everything to do with my behavior at The Foxy last night. But what could I have done differently? Everything, probably.

I should've just left when the crowd from Dawson's came in. Of course, I didn't notice Chris in the mix at first. All I noticed? Nick wasn't there.

Chris should never have made his way over. And Penny! She was flirting with him. I was only trying to protect her by pulling her away. Only he'd be dumb enough to think I was jealous. It wasn't until he had me cornered, trying to explain there was nothing between him and Shandy when I got mean. I really don't like my mean self. Initially, all I said was I didn't give a shit about his love life. But when he shouted out to my friends I was only into married men, I felt all the days of no phone calls unleash. I slapped him.The entire bar went quiet as he walked out of the bar. Linda was the first one to speak, "I'm not sure we should slap our customers."

So now I will paint on cheery smile on my face and attempt to prove to Ginny I'm a worthy hire. And pray she doesn't listen to office gossip.

Pulling up a chair to Ginny's desk, I'm focused on work. Ready to learn the loan process.   "Your customers will no longer be the elderly or the affluent," she tells me. "Unless, of course, they're cosigning a note for their kids."

I inform Ginny of my amusement over waiting on people this summer. And how quickly I came to realize the impossibility of distinguishing a millionaire from a pauper. On numerous occasions, I informed customers, wearing mud-caked boots and ratty clothes that their checking balances exceeding $50,000. "I should be okay then," was a common response. I wanted to shout, "Go buy a couple of cars! Write a check!" On the other side of the coin, I was shocked to learn of well-known professionals struggling with overdrafts.

"There's something else," Ginny says to me. I spot the look of a judge in her eye. Here it goes. The talk about my behavior. "It's rewarding when you help someone purchase a home or a car they really want, but it can be tough at times. Like when you have to deny a loan or even worse, collect on one."

I nod. And breathe a sigh of relief. So far, I haven't been caught breaking curfew.

The morning flies by as she shows me how to prepare loan documents for an upcoming closing. Then she asks me to lunch. I learn she is from Perling! That magical place called Perling. I want to ask about Nick, but I don't. After all, I'm trying to forget him. She seems intent on talking about careers.

"I considered getting my MBA, but once I got my bachelor's, I just wanted to be married. Two kids later, my MBA seems far-fetched."

"Do you have any regrets?" I ask.

She puts her fork down. "My life is pretty great. I could use a smidge more help around the house. And I wonder about more—"

"More what?"

She shakes her head. "An MBA might've helped me, but maybe not. If you have a chance to become a commercial lending officer, do it. I'll get you some experience this summer. You'll need that if you ever want to become a president."

I smile. "Well, okay then."

After lunch, we head to the board room for a loan closing. Twelve plushy chairs wrap around a large granite-topped table. Ginny opens the green brocade drapes to let more light in, calling attention to the particles of dust floating in the air.

Once we're organized, Penny raps on the door, leading in the customers for the closing. Penny winks at me, making me feel slightly relieved about the events of the night before. Then Ginny introduces me to Judy, who wears Mickey Mouse scrubs, and Jim who wears crisp trousers and a plaid shirt. I know from the loan docs she's a nurse and he's a pharmacist.

"Amy's a summer intern from the U of Iowa," Ginny explains. "Do you care if she observes our closing?"

"Of course not. Especially since she's a Hawk," Jim says with an awkward laugh.

"Hawk fans?" I ask.

"Went to pharmacy school there," Jim says. "Judy's a Hawkeye by marriage."

Ginny presents all the documents and points to five thousand signature lines. When she leaves to make copies, Jim refuses the notion of silence.

"Jude's becoming a nurse practitioner," he says. "The reason for the refinance. In addition to the lower interest rate."

"Awesome!" I say, even though I already know this. "Any kids?"

"One so far," Judy adds while Jim pulls out a photo. "I need to do this before anymore come along." As Ginny returns to the office, she adds, "Ginny understands."

"Definitely."

"Amy's probably not too worried about kids just yet." Jim swivels his head to me. "Are you? I guess I shouldn't assume anything."

"Oh gosh no!"

I observe Ginny with her customers. She seems to be making their day, even educating them on the more mundane aspects of their loan. Could this be something I want to do for the rest of my life? A career in finance?

I was swayed to travel down this path because of the image. I like the idea of me wearing suits, pulling down a gratifying check, bossing people around. It would make up for the fact that perhaps I don't really love numbers all that much. Now, I'm seeing how the job actually impacts people. Maybe it wouldn't be such a bad gig after all. I wonder if they'd let me sing to them.

CHAPTER 18

IN HEAVEN THERE IS NO BEER

JULY 4, 1992

Lyn and I pave our way to Perling's Annual Parish Picnic to celebrate the Fourth of July. No one celebrates our independence quite like German Catholics.

We're discussing Lyn's more frequent contact with Mitch as I notice the large sign promoting "Gottes Land." Parked cars swarm on the ten or twelve streets making up the town.

"Probably just a summer fling," Lyn says casually.

"I hardly see you on weekends anymore," I say. "Must be a teensy bit serious?"

"Define teensy."

"You know, this town really is a charming little hamlet of a place," I say to Lyn as I check out the residences. "Look at those cute flower pots." I glance at Lyn who rolls her eyes at me.

"The tricycle in that tree is nice," she points out.

Old two-stories intersperse with newer ranch-styles. Most have white siding and colorful petunia-ish beds bordering the entrances. Hot wheels and bicycles compose the majority of a few yards. Many vehicles choose to set outside of their garages. There are some quirks in this community.

"Do you think it could work?" Lyn asks as she expertly parallel parks her Colt.

"What?"

She kills the engine, then rests her head on her hand, giving me a "crazy-bitch" look. "Uh...Mitch and me? The guy we've been talking about the entire way here."

"Oh yeah." I refocus my thoughts. "Definitely! I think. But you know...guys are just so fickle. And there's the long distance issue. Unless you're willing to move. Did you say you're willing to move?"

"Thinking about Nick? Wondering if he's here?"

I shake my head. "No way. I couldn't care less."

We walk to the picnic area, filled with make-shift stands of kid games, homemade crafts, food, and one of the primary reasons we are here: the beer garden. There is no age group that defines this event. The crowd is infiltrated with the elderly, middle-aged, young parents with children and babies, and, of course, college kids (or rather, young adults). Even though I didn't grow up in a German colony, I can't help but become caught up in the community pride these picnics evoke. Everyone seems to be working so hard with a sense of purpose and yet so happy about it. Maybe it's the beer.

After proudly flaunting our IDs to the rent-a-bouncers outside the beer garden, we find a few friends from high school.

Time evaporates as we catch up on each other's lives. Nicole has taken a job with Principal Insurance in Des Moines. She even seems excited about such a job. Lisa starts Med School at Creighton this fall. Dee Ann has one more semester before she graduates with her Fine Arts degree. Her semester in Spain last spring keeps us captivated with spicy tales from Madrid. And after everyone takes a turn at elaborating on their latest romances, they face me.

"Since Lyn has stolen my boyfriend from Iowa City, I got nothing," I say.

Dee grabs my arm and lays her head on my shoulder. "You might be in luck. Guess who I spot at the beer counter?"

Everyone does an about-face to look through the crowd, except me. I wonder if Dee has heard about Nick Klein.

"It's your homeboy, Chris! Maybe you two can sing a duet for us?"

I give her a fierce squinty-eye. "No chance."

Nicole pipes in, "Yeah. He hasn't weathered so

well."

"I think his new look is cute," says Lisa. "Kinda like grunge meets Loam County."

"It's not for me," I say. "However…" I glance at Lyn who knows my regret at slapping him the other night. "I probably at least owe him an apology."

Everyone grows quiet. So we all take a sip of beer at nearly the same time. That's when I feel a pinch at my side. Spinning around, my heart bounces on the pavement as I see the baseball uniform before me, along with those coffee-brown eyes–looking more intense than ever.

"Amy Gaer," he says. "Did you come to watch the ball game today?"

I hear one of my friends utter, "Isn't that Nick Klein?"

I shake my head. "Just got here."

"Hey Axland," he addresses her lightly. "Crushed two out of the park today."

"Only two?" She holds up her beer, as if she's checking the breeze. "With this wind blowing to the north?"

Nick shrugs then asks my group of friends who needs a beer. As the rest of my group confirms their thirst, I reject the offer. "Definitely not for me. But thanks anyway." He strides away to the beer stand.

"Alright, Amy," Dee Ann asks. "What's up with Nick Klein? Isn't he married?"

I shift in my sandals. Then Lyn comes to my

rescue. "They met at a bar after his wife left him. Had one date, ran into his wife. He hasn't called since."

"He's cute," Lisa says. "Has my vote."

"Looks like a class reunion!"

It's Chris, joining our circle by wrapping his arms around Nicole and Dee Ann. Everyone greets him warmly, and for once he avoids my eyes. They all chat, catching him up with their current whereabouts as I stand, shifting about, with Lyn nodding me on, giving me a look which says, "Here's your chance."

I force myself in the circle. Among the crowd, I notice Penny and her boyfriend. She waves, and I wave back. She notices me approaching Chris and gives me a questioning look.

"Chris, do you have a minute?" I ask.

He glances over his shoulder, but doesn't look me in the face. "You gonna slap me again?"

"I'll try not to."

He follows me a short distance away from our friends.

"I just wanted to apologize," I say. "I really do feel bad about slapping you."

He nods, then looks past me.

"You know, we were pretty good friends once," I add. "And I always thought maybe we could be friends again. But you just wouldn't let it die. Let us die."

He faces me. "I think the slap did it."

I see Nick returning with a beer for everyone. He glances at me and Chris. Part of me wants
to hurry up this conversation. "I guess that's good,
right?" I ask, trying to get a smile from my ex.

"I hate that you think so lowly of me now." His
head drops and he stares at the ground. "I know I
made mistakes."

"High school romances don't last Chris. You
knew I never wanted to stay around here."

He looks over to Nick. "Really?"

I notice Penny, creeping towards us. "Hey. See
that girl over there with the pink glasses?" I point
her out.

"Your drinking buddy? The one with the big
boyfriend?"

"I think she likes you," I say. "And from everything I hear, her boyfriend's kind of a jerk."

"And I'd be a real step up?" He finally looks
directly into my eyes. And for the first time in a long
time, I remember the old Chris that used to make me
laugh. I crack a hint of a smile.

"I think you would, Chris." I pat him on the
shoulder. "I'll put in a good word for you at work."

He glances over to Nick. "Yeah, well," Nick
takes a long drink of his beer. "I'd put in a good word
about you to Nick. But I don't think I need to."

Then Chris smiles at me sadly, and walks back
to his crowd of friends. I think I've just finally said
goodbye to Chris Fekes. But I've thought that before.

I inch my way back over to the group who has

been recently supplied with beer by Nick. He offers me a bottle.

"Trying to get me drunk, are you?"

"Doesn't appear you need any help at this point." He flashes a way-too-charming glance at me. "Hope I'm not interfering with anything." As he points to Chris, a hand grabs my shoulder. It's Judy from the loan closing.

"Amy, right?" Judy asks. "Did you go to school with my brother here?"

Loam County is a microscopic world.

"Sort of. I was a freshman when he was a senior."

Judy nods, as it seems to occur to her she's walking into a budding romance.

"So…" Judy asks. "How'd you two meet up?"

I take a drink.

"Amy's a huge baseball fan," Nick says. "Follows the Perling town team."

"Where's Jimbo?" Nick asks Judy, switching the subject.

"My dear husband is allowing me to have one beer while he takes Josh on a few more rides. Isn't he great?" She tilts her head and points. "That didn't last long. Here they come. Apparently, I'll only get to drink half a beer."

"Amy from the bank." Jim extends his hand to me as he holds a minion of a boy in his other arm. The only noticeable difference between the two is that Jim's hair is receding and Josh sports a full head of dark waves. The toddler reaches for Judy. As she grabs for him, he digs his head into her shoulder.

"Want to come to me, Joshy?" Nick asks.

"No," Josh emphatically replies.

"I have some M&M's."

Josh considers the idea, then reaches for Nick.

"Bribery. Works every time. Works better if you actually have something to offer." He looks at me. "Want to join me and buy some candy for my nephew? Give Judy and Jim some alone time?"

"Alone time at the Perling picnic," Judy says. "If that's not beautiful, I don't know what is."

We head toward the food and kiddie stands as Josh shyly steals a few glances my way.

"Do you like Spiderman?" I ask the chubby face, digging into Nick's shoulder.

He looks down at his shirt and tries not to smile. Then he he puts two fingers out for me.

"Peace!" I say, showing him the peace sign back.

"He's telling you that he's two years old," says Nick.

"Oh! You're two! How awesome is that!"

"You'll be three in September, big guy," Nick reminds him.

"Is Josh your only nephew?"

"For now. My other sister, Jonie, is expecting in November."

In addition to buying M&Ms, we take Josh on

a few kiddie rides like barrel cars and the bouncy house. We swing by stands like duck races and pop bottle throw contests. I'm holding two stuffed animals and cotton candy as we head back to the beer garden. I focus on walking straight and talking without a slur, since we are essentially chaperoning. It all feels very odd though. Walking around with a married man, who's coddling an adorable toddler... not to mention I'm quite buzzed.

Relief washes over me when we return with Josh. There's this voice in my head, that sounds an awful lot like my father, telling me I should go home.

"Jude's downed two beers since you guys left," says Jim. "So I best be getting my bride and trophy home."

Judy eyes him with playful disgust. "Nice. Can you for once speak like a normal person. Forget you're from Loam County? You are a professional, remember?"

As I watch them leave the crowd, I tell Nick, "You're family seems really nice."

Nick shrugs. "They're okay."

"I should get going."

"Already?"

"I work tomorrow. The fifth of July isn't a bank holiday."

Nick hesitates a moment. "Can I take you home?"

I bite my lip. "I don't know, Nick. I came here with Lyn."

"Please?" He asks pleadingly with those hypnotic eyes. Damming eyes. "I promise I won't try anything."

I tell Lyn I'm leaving.

As we walk out together, he places his hand on my back, they way he did the first time we met. I feel nervous, elated, dizzy. We climb into his old Ford pickup and, before he starts the car, he turns to me.

"The divorce is final."

"Really?" I say, bouncing a bit in the seat. "So quickly?"

"We both waived the ninety-day waiting period. I found out on Tuesday and really wanted to call you, but thought I should wait a few days first."

He's been waiting for the divorce to become final, as a true gentleman would.

"How do you feel about it?" I ask.

He looks straight ahead. "Relieved. Really."

As Nick drives me to my house in Fox Plaine, a Van Halen marathon on the radio prompts a debate. Old Van Halen or new Van Halen?

"Not that I don't like new Van Halen. I do, but it's just not the same," I say with my voice rising.

"Sammy kicks David Lee Roth's ass," Nick says.

"Sammy might be a better singer than David Lee Roth. But the old music is way more provocative. Not so studio-driven. It's raw. Fresh. I just like how Eddie was so innovative at the beginning of his career."

"How can you say that old Van Halen is innovative? Half of their old songs are remakes."

"Touché," I say quietly.

"Did I make you mad?"

"Gosh no. I could talk all night about music."

"I wouldn't mind." Nick pulls into my driveway. "Would you like to continue this discussion? With me? Like maybe tomorrow night?"

"I think we *need* to continue this discussion."

But right now, you can kiss me if you want to.

We are quiet for a moment as we struggle to say goodbye. Nick pulls me to him and whispers, "The first time I saw you, you know what I thought?"

I shake my head.

"Beyond adorable. I thought to myself you were 'beyond adorable'."

Then he presses his lips against mine, softly. At first. Then, more, much more. I'm not sure I've ever felt a kiss with this much intensity. It compares to the fireworks which blast off in the background as Sammy echos the sentiments in my head. *Why can't this be love?*

CHAPTER 19
WOULDN'T IT BE NICE

JULY 1992

It's an unbearably hot and humid day in July. The act of breathing makes me sweat. The rank smell of cattle and hog yards waft over the entire county. Yet, I'm gleeful! I've seen Nick every day for the past two weeks now. We have determined to outsmart the uncomfortable weather with a visit to Plaine View Lake. Things always tend to happen at the beach.

So here we are, looking over the greenish-brown water. I spot a few rustic fishing boats bobbling in the distance. Our large blanket lays over the caky sand, while my toes hang over the edge, digging into the salty granules. I feel so sophisticated wearing my black J. Crew bikini (a hand-me-down from Jean) on this sparsely-populated beach which hosts only smattering of goose poop.

"Wanna swim?" I ask.

After a pause Nick says, "Okay."

I lift myself up while he stays grounded. Then he looks to me and says, "Just so you know, I can't swim."

"Can't swim? At all?"

He shrugs. "Red Cross isn't very considerate of planting season."

I grab his hand to pull him up. "I'll teach you! It's easy."

We step into the warm water, wading past mothers playing with toddlers in Mickey Mouse inner tubes and skinny boys doing flips off the floating dock.

Once we are submerged to our shoulders, I face Nick.

"Show me your doggie paddle."

He looks at me blankly.

I take his hands, guiding his arms back and forth in standard treading motion.

"Curl your legs up now, like a baby and use those strong arms to keep yourself above the water."

He splashes his arms around ferociously, bringing a fair amount of attention to us, while his head sinks under. After flying up and spitting out water he says, "Any other ideas?"

I work with him again, using various speeds and arm motions.

After thirty minutes of instruction, I decide either he is either unteachable or I'm quite possibly the worst swimming instructor in the world.

"You have an interesting density," I say with resignation. "We won't be calling you the unsinkable Molly Brown any time soon."

"I make for an interesting guy."

Nick pulls me closer. Then he lifts me high up in the air, as if I'm flying like an eagle. The air tingles on my wet skin, and exhilaration immerses me. I extend my arms out in flight, taking in the grandness of moment. That's when Nick launches me in the water.

I plunge under, swallowing half of the lake in my shock. Submerged for only a few moments, I burst through the water, gasping and coughing. "YOU! EVIL!"

"Sorry?" he says patting my back. "I am German."

After I gain my composure, I dive under water close to the sand, like a bottom-dweller, directly toward Nick's legs. I try to take him down. When he doesn't budge, I grab his trunks and pull them down. Then I swim away, reappearing about twenty feet away.

"And you are nothing but a wicked temptress," Nick says, adjusting them back on.

I wade back, tentatively, as I wipe the lake goo from my face.

"I'm not sure about you yet," he says with a sly

grin. He pulls me to him, not taking his eyes off me. He's nearing to kiss me. Then he lifts me up, only to dunk me. I resurface, grasping my drenched head.

With a lame attempt to apologize, he follows me as I stomp back to the blanket. I flash him a pouty smile, and he puts his arm around me. His touch has begun to dispel my pout.

Once we have stumbled our way back, I notice a clamor of people setting up down from us. I look twice to see Penny in the crowd.

"Hey!" I say. "Penny's over there. Wanna come over with me to say hi?"

Nick glances over to the group. "Maybe later."

"You sure?"

Nick gives me a curt nod, grabbing a Gatorade from the cooler.

I bounce over, waving to Penny, trying to get her attention. She stands next to her hulking guy with a cross tattoo on his shoulder.

"Hey Amy," says Penny as the guy turns around to face me. "Meet my Jeff."

"This the Amy you won't shut up about?" says Jeff as he takes off his muscle shirt.

Penny smacks Jeff in the arm. She shifts to one hip and lifts up her silvery visor. "Didn't you know? I'm obsessed with you. I think about you every night."

Jeff is looking at me, arms folded. "I don't see how her hair's any different than yours, Pen."

Penny shakes her head. "Nice conversation

starter, Jeff. Smooth." She looks to me. "I told him you had cute cut. I need to do something different with this frizzy shit."

"She's never happy," Jeff grabs hold of her. "If she ain't happy with her hair, it's something else."

I pull back my wet, stringy hair. "You could always dip your locks in the lake water. Gives it a nice, algae-like sheen."

Neither of them laugh at my attempt at a joke.

I look back to Nick. "It was nice to meet you Jeff," I say. "Better get back to my date."

"Is that Nicky Klein over there?" He says. "That dog didn't take long to find another squeeze. Didn't think he and Sarah would ever split up. Was kind of surprised to hear that."

Penny is shaking her head. "Well they did."

My smile falters. "I better get back. Before that dog finds a different squeeze."

But Jeff doesn't hear me. He has already turned back to his crowd.

"Catch you Monday, Amy," Penny says while shaking her head.

I wave to her while walking away. "Enjoy the rest of your weekend."

I tiptoe on the hot sand and settle back on the blanket next to Nick.

"Penny dates Jeff Gooden, huh?" Nick asks. "Too bad for her. She seems pretty cute for him."

"Really?" I say. "What do you know about Jeff? She moved from Omaha to be with him."

"Ridiculous." Nick rubs my shoulder. "Following someone to Loam County. Especially him."

"Not your favorite person?"

Nick doesn't respond.

"Was he in your class?"

He shakes his head. "Older. We were in FFA together." He looks to me. "Let's just say he is an arrogant fuckhead. Now he wants to be my agronomist. Calls me all the time to sell me chemicals. He'll never get my business."

Pretty strong words from Nick. It's the first time I've heard him talk this way about anyone, which makes me feel bad for Penny. Yet, it makes me feel better about Jeff's comments about Sarah. Methinks he was just trying to get under my skin, for some reason.

The sun is directly overhead at its highest point, baking a thin crust on my skin. I feel the moisture evaporating from my body, parching me. How can these UV rays, which are proven to cause harm, feel so delightful?

"FFA. Future Farmers of America!" I say, changing the topic. "Bet you looked all spiffy in your navy and yellow jacket."

He shakes his head. "I did not join to wear the jacket. Only in it for the farming."

"For the farming. Must've been nice always knowing exactly what you wanted to do."

He shrugs. "I never got a call from the Major League." He takes my hand and begins making circles on my palm with his fingers. "I thought about going to Iowa State. Figured it didn't make any sense."

Nick lays my hand down, keeping his hand loosely over it, then stares ahead at the water.

"Iowa State?" I say. "Good thing you didn't go. It never would've worked between us. How could I be with someone from my interstate rival?"

He juts his lip, then turns to me. "Not even for one summer?"

My heart stops. Just for one summer. Just for one summer.

CHAPTER 20

WE ARE FAMILY

JULY 1992

The Go Go's and I chant together while I drive to a baseball game in Perling. *Head over Heals. Can't stop myself.* It feels as if I'm outperforming Belinda Carlyle herself.

I miss Lyn's company. To think, she's opting yet for another weekend in Iowa City and I'm here. Jean's in Europe and I'm here. Yet, there's a particular lightness coursing through me as the summer breeze whips into my windows and the song thumps its bass line, sounding out a well-placed discord. My heart is elevated as I drive past the rows and rows of tall golden corn tassels. How pretty they appear!

I arrive at the game to find Nick's pickup markedly absent. So I beat him here. I try to wave to Brad so I don't feel completely awkward. He apparently doesn't see me.

Aside from the orange and blue uniforms making their presence on the field, the ballpark has a nostalgic appearance, with a railroad as a backdrop and seeming as if it hasn't changed in fifty years. The manual scoreboard sits in left field, faded from the elements. Weathered metal bleachers serve its small fan base. Some followers bring their own lawn chairs. A peeling shed, which served as a concession stand last time I was here, remains all locked up. Dang. I'm thirsty.

So I choose a seat next to a young woman with a cooler. After learning she's Brad's sister, Anna, I'm delighted to learn her cooler is full of beer. And she is gracious enough to share with me, especially since I'm attentive to her baseball stories involving Brad and Nick. I don't completely understand what's she telling me, but I smile and laugh like I do.

Soon the familiar Ford pickup pulls into the park and Nick, pulling on his jersey, hurries to the dugout. He catches my eye and hurtles me a grin which makes me levitate. Then he runs out to second base and relieves the high school kid playing the position, who trudges back to the dugout. Anna is rehashing the season thus far, and I think I hear something about how this has been a great distraction for Brad since their mother died. I offer my sympathy, but my focus is on the field. On Nick. He dances about the field, tossing the ball with his teammates as if they were rehearsing for a ballet.

Every time he moves, it's like watching the premier dancer, and I have to remind my heart to slow down.

My theater is interrupted when a Ford Explorer pulls in next to Nick's pickup. Judy and Jim emerge. Then another couple crawls out of the backseat with Josh. Since the lady is pregnant, I assume this is Nick's other sister Jonie. She is smaller, but pretty like Judy. Jonie sports a short haircut, while Judy's hair is long and noticeably blonder.

Jonie's husband leans toward the short side with no apparent neck. Wearing an oversized, untucked Nike t-shirt and jean shorts, I'm guessing he's more of a blue-collar guy. He contrasts with Jim in his polo shirt and plaid shorts. I'm feeling a little nervous to meet the family, since I'm positively buzzing by now. Two cans lay at my feet. Maybe I should've had a sandwich before I came. But I'm trying to avoid all possible chances of tummy bloat.

They spot me.

Here they come.

Judy introduces me to Jonie and Mike, who greet me warmly. Especially Mike. I think he might hug me. Jonie explains a due date in November, as if she needs to apologize for her large belly.

Mike asks where I got the beverage, eyeing the cooler, as if he already knows.

"Anna gave it to me." I point to her, but she is too preoccupied with the game to notice my hint. Thank God I didn't have a cooler along. They'd think Nick is dating a lush.

"Jim!" Mike says. "What do you say we run up to the Eddie's? For refreshments?"

"That does NOT sound good," says Jonie.

"We'll come right back," Jim says to Judy with his chin tucked under. "Promise."

"Come with us Joshy!" Mike says picking up his nephew. "We'll get you some candy and Mountain Dew."

"Don't think so Mike," says Judy. "My two-year old doesn't need to learn about the drinking rituals of the men of Loam County just yet."

Mike lets Joshy down, messing his hair. "Sorry your mom is such a fun-hater."

Judy raises her eyebrows at Mike who immediately adds, "Only kidding."

Then Mike and Jim leave in the Explorer as Nick's sisters and Josh sit next to me as the game starts. I feel slightly self-conscious about my alcohol-breath.

Sometime into the second inning, Josh shouts, "Grampa! Gamma!"

A gray Ford Taurus trawls into the baseball park.

My eyes widen as I quickly kick my beer cans under the bleacher. Jonie and Judy laugh at my action.

"Have you met Mom and Dad yet?" asks Jonie.

"No. As a matter of fact, I'm not sure they even know about me."

Jonie asks Judy, "Do they?"

Judy shrugs and says, "I never told them. And you know Nick."

The beer bile rises to my throat. Perhaps I should leave now. Did Nick know his whole family was going to be here?

Nick's parents get out of the car as Josh races toward them. My first impression? Disparity. Nick's Dad (who I know as Joe) is tall. Nick's Mom (who I know as Helen) is short. He is nearly bald. She has lots of white, curly hair. As they approach, I see how Nick resembles his father, especially in the eyes. I see how the girls resemble Helen with their petite frames. Helen seems to have a lively demeanor as she kisses and hugs her grandson. They are dressed exceptionally well for a ball game in their gabardine shorts and cotton button-down shirts. The couple brings a sort of presence that seems almost too formal for the game.

Judy provides her parents a quick recap of the inning and scores. Then Jonie decides to drop the bomb.

"Mom? Dad? Have you met Nick's new friend, Amy?"

I smile and wave, as they give me a examining look which seems to last five minutes.

"Nick has mentioned you," Helen replies. I'm not sure whether to feel relieved, until she adds, "I told him to bring you by the farm."

Joe pipes in with his gravelly voice. "He's probably afraid we'll put you to work!"

I think he's joking, so I attempt to quip back.

"That doesn't scare me."

When you drink beer, sometimes things don't come out right. Like that last response, apparently. They are quiet, and I feel stupid.

"I mean, well, I wouldn't mind, helping and all. It's probably pretty interesting, raising pigs and cows. And sheep. And corn. And everything else."

Shut up now, Amy.

"Didn't you grow up on a farm?" Joe asks as if it's a character flaw.

"No, but I always wanted to!" I don't know why I said that. It's not really true. "My Dad bought me a horse when I was younger, and we kept her at a stable." That is true, but I'm not going to tell him we eventually sold the horse for an Atari.

"Acht. Horses. Nothing but fence-wreckers. Stupid animals."

I'm beginning to wonder if Joe's upset with me.

"Dad would never let us get a horse no matter how much Jonie and I begged," Judy says.

"Hell, you had a dog already. Caesar was almost big enough to ride."

"Caesar never took to a saddle," Jonie responds evenly. I can't really tell if she's joking.

The more we visit, the more I realize Joe uses the same gruff demeanor whether he's talking with Josh or commenting about a call in the game. But even if he isn't upset with me, I'm still intimidated.

Scared shitless actually. Helen is more soft-spoken. But she seems to hold her own with Joe, debating him on three calls.

Apparently, the Klein family are baseball aficionados. Perhaps because Joe, I learn, was a pitcher in the minor leagues. A bit ignorant in this subject, I step into the rhythm of the family by grumbling at the same calls they do and by cheering at the plays they cheer at. The only thing I really know about this particular game is the score and that Nick looks very fine in his suit.

The game ends and Perling wins six to two. Brad brushes by, over to Anna, giving me a smile and a nod before walking off to meet other teammates. I shout "Nice game" to him, but he is out of sight, acting as if he didn't hear me. I feel slightly brushed off. But not for long. Nick swoops in from out of nowhere with two other baseball players, twins, whom I know from high school.

"Thanks," Nick says, as if I was talking to him. "You all met Amy? Hope you were somewhat nice to her. Dad especially."

"What?" Joe either didn't hear or didn't want to hear Nick's last statement.

"I think we know this girl!" one of the twins remarks. "She was one of those band girls! Am I right?"

"Sorry Amy. I've protected you from my cousins as long as I could. Jake and Will just got back from a tour overseas. The Gulf War. They're finishing school at Creighton now."

"The war," I say with indebtedness, exacerbated by alcohol. "Well, thank you. Thanks for serving."

They both flash a toothy smile. "You, my dear," says one of them, "are most certainly welcome."

Jake and Will ask me questions about myself and college. Even though they only graduated a year ahead of me in high school, I hardly know them since they ran in the sports circle. I'd really like to know what they did in Kuwait, but I stifle my curiosity for fear of hearing something disturbing. Then Joe begins to rehash the baseball game, and Jake is drawn into a lively discussion on missed opportunities.

"So you're a Business and an English major? I imagine you and Nick have pretty lengthy discussions on literature. Not." Will laughs at himself. Nick slugs him in the arm.

"Like you're Mr. Culture?" says Nick to Will.

"Probably more than you. I read stuff. Sometimes."

"Right," says Nick nodding. "Didn't you use my paper on *Animal Farm* in high school?"

"But you grew up on a farm. I knew you'd be an expert."

I giggle to myself. Then wonder if Nick would let me read his paper.

"Well," Nick admits to me, "I'm pretty sure

that was my sister's paper anyway."

So much for that idea.

Will looks at me and grabs my shoulder. "Hey, I was busy in high school. Had lots of parties to arrange. Not much time to write papers."

Jake turns away from his conversation with Joe, shaking his head. "You win, Uncle Joe. It was an error. My error."

Nick looks to the north. Hazy, bulbous clouds begin to hover. "I need to check my cows. Before this storm opens up." Then he looks to his cousins. "Coming over later?"

"Coming over?" Jake says. "Didn't Will tell you? We're moving in for a few weeks? Till school starts!"

"No," Nick says. "He did not tell me that."

"You could use the company. You know you love us." Jake gives Nick a bear hug. Nick pushes him away. "I'm out of here. Let yourselves in the house."

Nick turns to me. "Wanna check cows? With me?"

"Does it require skill?"

He grabs my hand and we are off on our next rural adventure. Before the storm comes.

CHAPTER 21

FOOL IN THE RAIN

JULY 1992

I'm riding in the pickup next to Nick on our way to check cows.

If anyone would've told me a a few months ago I'd be sitting here, I would've doubted the tale. What's more incredible? I'm more than content staring out this dusty window to observe the rolling, verdant countryside.

"Here we are." Nick parks his truck in front of a large steely-silver grain bin which sits amidst barns and machine sheds. Tractors and other types of equipment I can't identify are also strewn about. I strain to see the house, but it's somewhat hidden behind a grove of trees, located farther down the long lane we traveled to get here. He hasn't invited me inside yet. Maybe tonight.

"You ready?" he asks.

I nod with confidence, then hop out of the car to prove my enthusiasm.

"We have a little ways to walk," Nick says while changing out of his baseball cleats. "Might want to be careful where you step. Cow pie. Made daily."

We head around the largest machine shed to a path next to a cornfield away from the house. I'm trying to get a better glimpse of his house, but we veer off the path and continue on the north side of the grove.

We walk about a quarter of a mile on thick, tall grass. While my ankles are getting scratched up, the fresh, different air awakens my spirit. Big trees salute trees to my left and a happy bean field greets to my right. My beer buzz is fading because nature is clearing my head. Soon we approach a barbed wire fence where our path of long grass ends and a pasture begins. I grab the fence in between the barbs, pushing it down to step over it.

"Stop!" Nick shouts.

I pause, holding the fence.

"It's hot!" he says, holding his hands up.

"What's hot?" I ask, as he stands, not crossing.

"The fence?" he says, his face screwed up. "It's supposed to be anyway."

"You mean it's electric? I didn't think barbed wire fences were electric."

"Did you really grow up around here?" Nick asks as he walks to a post. He grabs a screwdriver stuck in the ground, and runs the end on the post and the wire. It snaps. He looks at me. "It is hot." Then he looks at my feet. "You must have amazing rubber on your shoes."

"The best. I made sure they'd hold through electric fence. Obviously."

Putting his hand to his head, Nick says, "God, I'm glad I didn't shock you. Would've hated to give that message to your dad."

We continue our journey up a small hill. Once we reach the top, we see a herd of black and brown cattle leisurely scattered on spotty grass amidst a sky decorated with looming, puffy clouds overhead. It's practically cliché.

"My bossies," Nick says. I notice his lips curve up slightly, a modest pride emerging from his face.

"Bossies?" I ask. "You have your own lexicon."

"Stay here so you don't spook them." Nick walks away confidently toward and through the cows, counting them off.

"I wasn't planning on scaring them," I say to myself.

They aren't spooked by him, but the bovines stare back at me. If their tails weren't swishing flies, many would pass for statues. Two calves catch my eye as they frolic together. Unknowingly, they edge closer to me. One takes notice, stares at me for no more than two seconds and quickly dashes away. The smaller of two chases down the other, then attacks. Then it turns around to run directly toward me. I calculate my getaway speed, but it spins around, prancing away soon enough, making my quick fear transition into a giggle. I'm entranced. Like when I'm reading a book. Or listening to a symphony.

Nick comes back with anxiety pinching his face.

"Everything okay?" I ask.

"A cow's calving right now and she's stuck. Must've have bred late 'cause I thought she was open."

Apparently a cow needs help.

"I need to get the puller." He looks around. "Why don't you come with me. Not sure if you'll scare the herd by standing here alone."

We tear off into quick jog. While I like to think of myself in shape, I'm doing my best to keep up with Nick. When we reach the machine shed, I wait outside to catch my breath. He comes out with a contraption that should scare the shit out of the cow.

Our journey back to the pasture has a dampened paced, because Nick's now holding equipment. Thank goodness. Although, I'm still clipping along plenty fast. Once we reach the area where I was left before, I stop and wish him luck, happy to rest. But he turns to me with different plans. "Come on. I may need your help."

When we reach the massive cow on laying on ground, she's heaving as if she's dying.

"See the hooves?" Nick approaches the rear of

the cow.

The cow moans and I move back toward her head, startled with each loud grunt.

"Easy," Nick instructs. "Go slow."

I tiptoe around this beast as Nick engages the puller. The cow flinches, jerks, and groans. Nick struggles to get the calf out, and does his fair share of grunting as well. After what seems like hours, but has only been minutes, Nick bears his feet down, pulling hard. The cow moans low and deep. I clench every part of my body, hurting for the cow. Nick stumbles back to allow the bundle of slippery legs fall to the ground.

A new life has befallen before my very eyes – a furry, wet, creature with four spindly legs and eyes too big for its oblong face. I love it.

The mother stands up, nuzzling her newborn to lick it clean.

"Spectacular," I say as we stand back to watch.

"I never grow tired of watching this," Nick says. "Of course, I'd prefer not to pull."

We watch the reddish-brown calf try to stand, fall repeatedly, and eventually succeed. She seeks out her mother's underbelly. Soon she is sucking. Nick explains that once the calf takes to her mother, all should be okay.

Nick turns to me. "We just pulled our first calf together."

Our first? Has he suddenly placed me in his future? Or, does he plan on having calves all summer?

I feel the first drops of rain fall onto my shoulders. The cows begin to move toward us, unnerving me. I grab Nick's shoulder.

With an amused smile, he asks, "You ready to go?"

"It's raining. And cows are coming after us."

Nick doesn't say anything, but nods. I can't decide if he's testing me or not. But we pivot back and take a stroll in the pasture while the rain drenches us. I forget the cattle behind us and take in the earthy, fresh smell.

"Should we walk faster? Or jog?" Nick asks.

An image of lovers walking through a rainy Paris street fills my mind. An Iowa pasture suddenly becomes romantic as well.

"No, walking in the rain feels nice."

When we arrive back in the yard, he looks up to the house. "I could use a shower before I take you back to your car."

I look down at my rain-drenched, muddy clothes. "So could I."

And that's how I get to see Nick's house for the first time. The only thing I really notice? The outside is painted yellow and white. Cheery. And the bathroom shower is small for two people.

CHAPTER 22
NEED TO KNOW

JULY 1992

"Good weekend?" Ginny asks me as I walk into her office while she shuffles through papers.

My head spins, thinking about the awesome aspects of the weekend – many of them involving Nick and his body parts. But I'm trying to remain level, in the bank, so I censor my chitchat.

"I helped to deliver a cow," I offer.

"Doesn't get much better than that."

"Met the parents."

"And I'm sure they loved you," she says sitting up straight, putting down her pen. "Now. Roger would like to visit with you this morning."

My eyes grow wide as she waves her hands off. "It's nothing to worry about."

"Do you have any concerns about my performance?"

"Not one." She stands up, drawing closer to me as if to tell me a secret. Then in a lower voice she says, "But can I give you some advice?" Before I have a chance to react she says, "Ask him when you're slated to learn the mechanics of commercial and agricultural lending."

"Wasn't that in the plans?"

She blinks at me. "We've had discussions. He's being a little bucky about this one. Doesn't think women are cut out for it."

I find myself doing the squint-stare along with Ginny. We're squinting together in female resentment. I'm not completely sure I buy what she's saying. It seems so 1953. But I nod cautiously, and turn around to leave for Roger's office.

***

"Tell me about your experience so far this summer," Roger begins as if he's kicking off a classroom lecture, his hands folded together, eyes fully attentive on me.

So I respond as if I'm taking an oratory test, detailing everything I've learned, giving ad nauseam praise to all the staff. The more I talk, the more his eyes seem to drift as if he's thinking about something else. Perhaps I overspeak.

"Sounds like everything is going well for you." He smiles in a fatherly way. "Ginny's a good mentor as well. She knows her stuff."

Here's my chance. "I'm anxious to understand commercial and ag lending as well."

Roger places his index fingers together. "You think you'd really want to borrow money out to farmers?"

The question catches me off guard me. First, I try not to focus on his incorrect grammar usage. (Shouldn't a president know how to distinguish borrowing and lending?) Secondly, it's the first time he's ever used a condescending tone with me. Of course, Roger and I don't mingle all that much. I swallow hard. Then I ask, "Isn't ag lending a critical part of community banking though? Maybe *the* critical part?"

He doesn't respond immediately, but turns toward the window, seeming to consider my question. I hate pauses. Silence disturbs me. I tap my thighs, playing a song on the invisible piano before me. Finally, he says, "The majority of our portfolio is commercial and agricultural. But I'm going to be honest. There are very few women in those areas of lending. Farmers just don't take to women very well."

I bite my lower lip, unsure what to say. Just as I open my mouth, to begin some babble, he turns to me and says, "But I have an idea on how to get you some exposure there. Not in direct lending, but some relevant experience anyway." Scooting his chair toward the desk, he leans toward me—with more animation than is usual for him. "Actually, I've got a problem. And I'd like to turn it into an opportunity for you. Just received word we're going to be examined by the FDIC soon. And to compound to that, I found Donna's resignation letter on my desk."

"Yikes," I say, as if I understand all the implications.

"You have a semester left at Iowa to get your business degree right?"

I nod.

"I realize you probably want to finish up your business degree at the U of Iowa, but Creighton also has an excellent business program. I have a buddy who sits on their board of regents."

"Creighton's pretty pricey," I say decisively.

"What if I were to offer you a real job?"

"Donna's job?"

He offers me a business card with Creighton's admission information.

"Jobs are scarce right now," he says. "It's only a thought. Everyone loves you here. You seem to like it here."

Before coming home this summer, the thought of not going back to Iowa City would never have occurred to me. But now things are different. I look around Roger's office. I look outside the window across the parking lot to the bakery – with the Dutch letters. I hear my pulse beat through my ears. An image of Nick flashes through my mind.

"I'm not sure," I say. "It's kind of a big decision. Give me some time to think about it?"

"Of course," he says. "We'd be flexible with your hours while you finish your degree."

"Thank you for the offer," I say. "I am flattered."

"I'll give you some time to decide Amy," he says as I rise to leave. "But I will need someone in Donna's position soon."

"I understand."

Leave the U of Iowa? For Creighton? For the bank?

Or would it really be for Nick?

Deep down, I know the answer.

CHAPTER 23

TELL ME TELL ME TELL ME

JULY 1992

"How was Europe?" I ask Jean over the phone.

"Fine."

"Fine? The heck with *fine!*" I shout.

After a considerable pause she confesses. "It was cool. Really awesome. I'm just tired. Anxious. Trying to get organized here in Chicago."

"Favorite country? Let me guess! France! You fell in love in Paris!"

"I didn't like Paris. Too dirty. And I certainly didn't fall in love. Germany, however, was my kind of scene. The Germans are so meticulous. I wish you could've seen the cathedrals. I know you're not particularly religious, but the artist in you would've shed a tear. Almost made me cry. Me. Maybe it was all the beer. I drank a lot of beer over there."

"But no dirty love story?" I ask. "Just a story of

tidy Germans and tear-jerking churches?"

"No dirty love story. But speaking of love stories, what's this about Mitch and your hometown friend? Is it true? I'm starting to feel old maidish." She pauses, and I consider how to approach my news. Nick. School. "When you come to visit me, maybe we need to step up our man search. Take it a bit more seriously."

Her words give me a pang. Not the man search stuff. The part about visiting her. This will be the first autumn in four years I won't be reunited with my college roommate.

"Anyway, how about your summer?" she asks. "Any more trips to Iowa City?"

"Actually just the one for Jon and Vic's party. I've been working at a bank here in town, so I'm busy most Saturdays." I pause. "And actually, I met someone."

"What do you mean you met someone? Like in Fox Plaine?"

"Somehow our paths had not crossed before this summer."

"Amazing. Do tell."

"He's cute. He farms. He's divorced."

I sense her amused expression over the wire. "Apparently, this is not a serious fling."

"Why would you say that?"

"A farmer? How's that gonna work out?"

"You haven't seen his ass."

"Go on."

"Of course, the first time I met him, he was in a baseball suit."

"Distorts the the cute-butt rating," says Jean. "So, what's with this divorced thing. Is he like in his forties or what?"

"Gross!" I say. "He's only a few years older. And he's just divorced. He was actually married when we met."

"You're not a marriage wrecker, are you?"

"I don't like to think so," I say before switching topics. "Hey, something interesting has come up. I have a decision to make, and I could really use your input."

"Wait until your married," she says. "If he doesn't respect that–"

"The bank's offered me a full-time job as a loan processor."

"Tricky commute from Iowa City, isn't it?"

"Here's the clincher. My boss wanted me check into Creighton to finish my business degree, which I was thinking was crazy, because of the price tag and all. So here's the thing. The admission's officer began to talk to me about their MBA program, since I have my Bachelor's already and a few business classes under my belt. She suggested forgetting about adding a finance degree. Just get my MBA. Of course, it would extend my studies for about a year. But their program is geared for working people with classes at night."

"Don't you have to take your GMATs to get in?"

"I'm scheduled next Saturday morning. A quick Kansas City trip."

"Do you think your salary could offset Creighton's price tag?"

"Probably not entirely," I admit. "But I'm hoping to get some financial aid."

I hear a tick over the phone line.

"I have to admit I'd be jealous," she says. "Getting your MBA. But promise me you wouldn't stay at that bank position forever. A waste of an MBA. And moving up in the ranks of a community bank seems disappointing."

"No doubt," I say, more bashfully than I intend.

We are both quiet for a moment.

"I still haven't decided. I want to make sure I'm making the decision for the right reasons. It's a lot of money to invest."

"Amy Gaer. Staying in her hometown," says Jean.

I look out the window to see thick, dark branches covered by a leafy maple tree.

"The scenery has improved enormously since I've been back."

Nick's Journal

September 12, 1989

THE BEST NEWS EVER.

She started off by telling me she wanted to become a teacher. I didn't say anything at first. First nursing school. Then all the other jobs. I reminded her of all that. Made her cry. She cries a lot. When I rubbed her back, she just ran to the bathroom. So I walked out the door to tinker on my tractors. But how was I supposed to know what to do?

She should've started out with the other news first.
She ran out the door shouting at me.
We're having a baby. Let me restate. A baby!

I can't help imagining teaching him (or her) to play baseball (or softball). So, now it makes sense. She wants to be a teacher to have her summers off. Can't hardly blame her for that.

CHAPTER 24
MY OWN WORST ENEMY

JULY 1992

Speeding on the jagged highway, I dash past the countryside in a whir to tell Nick the news. I fly past a few tractors, hoping the drivers aren't Nick. Or Joe. And once I pull into Nick's driveway, my heart falls with the absence of a Ford truck. So much for a grand entrance.

After a walkabout the house, I'm overcome with a desire to attack the astounding stench of... what is it? Stale beer? A house un-dusted or un-vacuumed for a month? I stack the newspapers and empty the beer cans which lay scattered about the living room and kitchen. After a bit of picking up, I scour the dishes, mainly knives and coffee mugs. Apparently, Nick, Jake, and Will survive on beer and cold meat sandwiches. I lay my Creighton letter on the table just so.

A strange, unusual feeling of domesticity

takes over me. I decide to make a meal. Rummaging through the cupboards, the only thing I find is Kraft macaroni and cheese. But when the outdated jug of milk pours out the consistency of cottage cheese, I decide to pull back on the idea.

So I sit and read the newspaper – every detail of the *Omaha World Herald*. My horoscope today is only three stars and says: *It's likely that positive changes are about to occur. Keep your faith strong.*

Finally a vehicle pulls in the driveway. I coach myself to act cool, crossing my legs to keep them from bouncing as I sit here at at the kitchen table.

As the door slams shut, I shout, "Surprise! It doesn't stink in here! Too much."

Brad and another face appear at the door. The other guy, much slighter in stature, wears pressed plaid shorts and a bright orange polo.

"How'd that happen? Did Klein flush the toilet for once or what?" says Brad.

I shake my head. "Just cleaned. I just cleaned, that is."

"Nick hire you as his house cleaner?" he asks.

"Somehow I doubt I'll get paid for this," I say.

"Way beyond the call of duty," says the other guy, with a warm smile. "I'm Jim Claussen by the way. You must be Amy?"

"Claussen Farms?" I ask. I point to Brad. "Your Claussen's Farms?"

"The place I'm employed, if that's what you mean," says Brad. "He's my boss."

Jim shakes his head. "My dad is his boss. Not me. We were just gonna grab Nicky tonight since I'm back, but maybe he already had plans?"

"We really didn't make plans," I say. "I was just going to surprise him. But I don't know where he is."

"I think he had to bail hay first," Brad says.

"Oh, that's right," I say as if I knew. "I should probably leave."

"Don't go because of us," Jim says. "You're welcome to join us. Brad will behave."

"I don't know," says Brad looking at Jim. "If Amy comes, people will think we're on a double date with those fucking clothes you're wearing."

"Don't listen to him," says Jim as he digs through the fridge, grumbling about a beer.

"Thanks for the offer," I say. "But I probably can find other things to do tonight."

Woolfie will appreciate my company.

As I grab my letter and sneak it back into my purse, I hear the distinct roar of Nick's Ford. Within a few minutes, Nick stumbles through the door – holding a towel soaked with blood around his head. I rush to him, Jim stepping behind me. Brad remains motionless, hawing how the sight of blood makes him woozy. Nick begins to pull the towel off as blood gushes out.

"I was pulling a board off one of our sheds. Slipped. Hit my head."

Jim twists his face. "Looks like your brain is seeping out."

"Emergency room?" I ask in a panic.

"Tired of that fucking place," says Nick abruptly. "Just got stitches in my thumb a few months ago."

"I'll drive," Jim offers. "Amy? Brad? Want to ride along?"

I nod. "Absolutely."

"Not much I can do," says Brad. "Meet up with you guys at the bar later?"

"Don't blame you, Brad," says Nick. Then he glances to me. "No one really needs to come along. I could probably drive myself."

"Shut up, you martyr," says Jim. "Let's go. Before he convinces himself he doesn't need stitches."

I sense Nick doesn't want me tagging along to the hospital, since he's hardly given me a glance since arriving. Maybe he's just embarrassed. I wave off my insecurity in the name of helping him. He is, after all, bleeding profusely from the head.

CHAPTER 25

WARNING TRACK

JULY 1992

The nurse definitely had a crush on her ER patient.

Looking like a mental patient with a large bandage wrapped around his head, Nick sits on his couch as I say goodbye to Jim.

"Jim's a nice guy," I say, cuddling up to Nick. "One of your buddies from high school?"

"Yep. Part of the Claussen empire. He was too smart to stick around here." Nick gingerly lays his head back. "Works in Kansas City as a lawyer now. Doesn't make it back too often. I think he's here for a family reunion this weekend. Or something like that."

"Sorry your night was ruined."

He shrugs. "Maybe I'll feel better later."

"I have some news," I say, "that might perk you up."

"Really? You didn't just come over to clean my house?" Nick forces a smile while holding his head.

"I'm definitely not going to make cleaning your toilet a habit."

He puts his hand up for a high five. "I'm right with you. Gross business."

Grabbing the letter from my purse, I present the document as an award. "Read this."

"Creighton?" he asks, jutting out his lip. "What's this about?"

"Read it!"

Nick doesn't blink, nor does he move, as he reads. I'm expecting some joy to creep across his face any minute. He puts it down. Then he lifts it up and begins reading it again.

"This sounds like you got accepted into Creighton's MBA program. Like you would be transferring," he says without looking up. "Why? Why did you do this?"

Taking back the letter, I feel sheepish by his tone. Afraid to respond.

"The bank offered me a job in the loan department..." As I explain the story to Nick, his eyes don't waver. His jaws tighten. Finally, he interrupts me,

"You didn't apply to this program because of me did you?"

"Not exactly," I say quietly. "Would it have been so horrible if I did? Beside, I'm not even sure if I'm going to do it. But they offered me a research assistantship, which I didn't expect–"

"Good. You should think twice," he says with a sigh. "I wouldn't make any decisions because of me. Or any decision that gets you stuck here in Loam County."

I scoot away. "But I'd be stuck with you, pursuing an MBA. An MBA! And getting real job experience at the same time."

His voice rises. "But what kind of opportunities are you gonna get from working at a local bank? Head teller?"

I feel my ears burning. "Maybe I won't stick around." I stand up to leave.

"Hey, wait. Don't leave mad." Nick stands up, wobbling a bit. "I just don't want you to stay here. For me."

"I'm not sure how to interpret that."

"I thought this was just kind of a summer thing. Nothing serious."

"Goodbye Nick," I utter, marching out the door. He doesn't try to stop me.

I get in my car and drive away as fast as I can, with tears blurring my vision. I didn't want to come home. Now I don't want to leave. But the reason I don't want to leave doesn't want me to stay.

CHAPTER 26

WHERE BROKEN HEARTS GO

JULY 1992

Not one piano room open this morning. Iowa City is punishing me for my impending betrayal.

So, here I sit, on a quiet Sunday morning, pouting next to the music building, digging my feet into the bank of the Iowa River. Even though the grass is dry and prickly, my space here at least gives me solitude. Ducks, please stay away.

I check the time, wondering how much time I should give Mitch and Lyn to say goodbye. Screw it. Why am I being so graceful? Lyn's moving to Chicago soon anyway. Who'da thought she'd get all ambitious? Enrolling in DeVry. Love was good for her.

It was a disaster for me.

Now I'm on the verge of living and working in the my hometown. To get an MBA. And MBA! Me! Amy Gaer. At least Mom seems more impressed with the idea. Even if its not law school.

I turn on my stomach to stare at Hancher Auditorium. So much for sneaking in any more music classes.

How stupid.

All for a boy.

I need to get over him.

How did I let myself fall so quickly anyway? Could it have been the baseball uniform? No. I saw lots of baseball uniforms that night. There was something more.

Like the way he'd call me "beyond adorable."

Or how he'd shift about whenever I'd give him a compliment. Modesty can be so beautiful.

Maybe my infatuation was built on boredom.

Then why do I feel so badly?

A tap on my shoulders makes me flip around. A shadow blocking the sun announces, "Amy Gaer, the headbanger."

"Paul? Paul!" I leap to hug him. "You got my message last night!"

My lunge knocks him to the ground and I find myself on top of him, face to face. "You're still here! I was hoping you hadn't left for New York yet." We teeter back up, so my friend doesn't have to feel uncomfortable with my breasts pressed against him.

"New York isn't ready for me yet." He straightens himself up, brushing off the grass from his black tee. "I accepted a fellowship. Starting grad school this fall."

"A fellowship? You didn't tell me you applied!"

"We can still carry on our banter next semester," he says. "Our so-called debates. Unless business school makes you completely uninteresting."

I fall back on the hard ground, in one melodramatic sigh.

"What's going on with you?" Paul asks. "Your message last night was fairly incoherent. Couldn't tell if it was your small town wearing off on you, or the number of shots you drank." He faces me to see if I react. "Went to Prairie Lights this morning to see if by chance you'd show up, like your message mentioned. When you weren't there, I became curious. I don't normally go out of my way, but I thought I'd try your sanctuary." He points to the music building." That's when I saw this lithe figure sitting by the river bank. Didn't want you to go all Virginia Woolf on me."

"Just confused. Kind of sad."

I continue to explain my story, jilted love and all.

Paul nods his head, digging his hands into the ground. "Well you know what I say?"

"What do you say, Paul Rogers?"

"Fuck business school. Study music, like I told you before."

I press my hands into my head. "I've carved my path now."

"You can change it. It's not like you're on your death bed or anything. What are you 22?"

"I want a paycheck," I say. "If I do anything

differently, it'll have to be law school. Or my mother will shit."

Paul shakes his head. "I hope she shits anyway. Required bodily function." He takes my hand and pats it. "Business. Law. Neither are guarantees of a good or satisfying job."

"True." I bolt up. "Maybe I *should* go back to pursuing my rock star dream!" I pull my hair back. "Maybe I just didn't try hard enough."

"In terms of rock stardom, you suffer from an image problem."

"You think I'm ugly?"

"God no! You're as cute as a button. And that won't fly in the rock world. Do you even remember what you wore to those auditions? Baggy jeans, sweatshirts. Hair in a ponytail."

I shrug.

"I bet every one else was in leather or spandex."

"And to think. I've given up all that fame and fortune."

"When I say you should pursue music, I don't mean become the next Axl Rose, or even the next Madonna. There are other musical careers."

I smile. "Paul Rogers. I like how you dream. But you know what?" I begin to pull the grass out. "I'm probably stuck. I'm stuck in my hometown with my parents for the next year, at least. If I don't get my MBA, my mom will make sure I get my butt into law school. Creighton has a good law school."

Paul nods, and puts his arm around me. "I went to New York you know. This summer, just to see. When I got there, I was adrenalized. Caught up in the hustle of the city. Then when I unpacked my things, I looked out that tiny, crappy little window. And I knew it wasn't right." He looks at me. "Grad school is where I belong right now."

"I don't know where I belong."

"Things aren't always going to be perfect, but deep down you always know the right thing to do." Paul releases me, and hops up. Then he looks down at me. "You look good. Love sickness serves you well. Call me if you come back."

And he is off as quickly as he came. I sit up, feeling more confused then enlightened by his last words. What I thought felt right, was completely wrong. When I thought serendipity was pulling me through some awfully plushy clouds, lightning struck.

I look at my watch. It's time to go home. Back to Loam County. Damn Loam County.

CHAPTER 27

MOVING ON

AUGUST 1992

"Sorry about last night," I say to Penny on my way out to lunch.

"We've all had our share of heartbreaks," she says. "I'm getting tired of Karaoke anyway."

"Thank God for The Mothers. They know how to fill the silences," I say. "Can't wait to try out that killer tater tot casserole recipe."

"I know you make fun of us, talking about food all of the time. But it beat the hell out of you crying over the microphone."

I nod in agreement and leave Penny to her phones.

Forget Africa. If Bono would've heard me attempt *With or Without You* last night, he would've found a new kind of injustice to pursue. I shouldn't go out drinking with my coworkers in my current state of gloom.

As soon as I reach the bank exit, a familiar figure appears before me.

"Brad!" I say while holding the door for him. "How are you?"

"Haven't seen you at a game for awhile," he says, almost shyly.

I look away. "Been busy. You probably know already, but Nick and I aren't dating anymore."

His face awakens as if I was his alarm clock. Apparently, he hadn't heard.

Brad scratches his chin. I'm still waiting for him to pass through while holding the door, but he remains in place.

"Sorry to hear that. You going to lunch right now?" he asks. "Mind if I join you? After I drop off this deposit?"

I'm caught. Why can't I think of an excuse? I look down at my book.

"Or, did you have a date with that book?" he asks, stretching to read the title. "To Kill a Mockingbird?"

He probably wouldn't understand how I would just assume read another chapter in one of my favorite books of all time, even though I'm only reading it again upon the recommendation of my mother—another sneaky attempt to keep law school a viable option.

I look into Brad's expectant eyes. And smile.

"Lunch sounds great."

A diversion that somewhat connects me to Nick seems like a soothing, yet tortuous idea. I can hardly understand my consent. It's kind of like pressing on a bruise.

The longer I stand here and wait for Brad, the more I regret my answer. Will he get the wrong idea? Like, I'm attracted to him?

Too late now. Brad returns. With a grin to match a rodeo clown. Well. At least I made some-one's day today.

"Hey, can you drive? My car's a mess. And it ac-tually smells kinda like cow shit."

I laugh, because it feels better than crying.

Then he points to his clothes. "And I'm not really dressed for anything real fancy. Is Burger King okay? It suits my wallet."

Of course.

***

Brad and I are sitting in a booth, surrounded by windows. He's devouring a double whopper as I nibble on some horribly cold french fries. Unfortu-nately, Brad forgot to get cash at the bank in his hurry, so I sprung for the greasy lunch. He did feel embarrassed, and since I believe in equal rights, it didn't really bother me. Obviously. As I plan to tell this story to everyone this afternoon.

The worst part of the lunch has been the odor. Beyond the deep-fat fried walls, Brad emanates a bit of a cattle yard smell. So I find myself breathing through my mouth. But other than that, the lunch date hasn't been bad, since I've had to talk very little. Brad has taken care of that.

"Anyway, I go back to school next week myself. Maybe we could do something together this weekend... if you'd like or want."

Brad's words begin to fade as my eyes focus on the driver of a rusty Ford pickup, waiting in the drive-up lane. Nick. His hair already seems longer, and he's not looking any worse for it. Something makes him turn my way and our gazes connect for what seems to be a half of a millisecond. His expression changes slightly when he recognizes my lunch date. He looks away and drives forward.

"I'm sorry, Nick. You were saying..."

"Brad. You're with Brad."

"Brad. I know. Sorry. I'm busy this weekend. Lyn and I made some plans already. In Iowa City. Maybe some other time?" I offer lamely, lying through my teeth.

"I have three tickets to the Def Leppard concert in Kansas City in September," Brad tells me with his mouth full. I immediately tense up with the impending invitation as I think about Nick's expression. Was he jealous? "Part of their *Adrenalize* tour. My sister and I are going. My older brother was going, but can't now. Maybe you'd like to go with us?"

"I'm not sure." Or was Nick's expression of indifference?

"Don't you like Def Leppard?

"I love Def Leppard, actually." Or was it disgust? Maybe he was disgusted. "I've seen them twice in concert."

"You should come with us. It'd be a blast."

There's a small part of me that feels some satisfaction. I'm glad Nick saw me moving on.

"I'll think about it Brad. Maybe."

But mostly? I still feel heartbroken.

Nick's Journal

October 18, 1975

Dear Diary,

The worst day ever. Dave was in a very very bad accident. Lois died. She was pretty and nice to me. Mom and Dad are at the hospital right now because Dave is having a surgery. Jonie and Judy and I have to wait at home I guess.

I feel very sad. When I fought with my brother, we didn't really fight. I admire him. He teaches me stuff. Like how to throw curve balls. I don't know if I will ever be able to pitch like Dave. But I want to make him proud now.

I hope he will be okay.

CHAPTER 28
THE MUSIC IN ME

AUGUST 1992

"This will be like a doggie Disney World for you," I say to my puppy who's digging his terrier claws into my lap and pawing at the window. As we wind through the path to my grandmother's trailer, spruce trees loom around us as we inch our way deeper into this grove outside of Rockport. "This part of Missouri is a haven for wildlife."

"Will she ever move?" Mom asks my dad.

"She always says, 'not til someone carries me out.'"

As we pull into a small clearing I spot my grandma, in her rolled up jeans and a faded screen-printed t-shirt. She stands outside of her trailer next to a small tin building holding a cat. Other cats and kittens dart around her feet. She waves big, motioning for us to come to her.

Woolfie leaps out and tears around the yard, tracking the cats.

I skip through the tallish grass to hug her. Her hair has grown even longer, past her shoulders, and her waist has thickened. As we embrace, I notice all the wood piled up on the side of the trailer.

"Ready for the winter, Grams?"

Glancing back she says, "Hope so." Then she whispers, "Probably don't need that much. But chopping wood's how I keep my trim figure." Then she looks to me and my mother. "Now, do you two ever eat? Good thing I'm cooking today. But first I gots to show ya my new baby!"

I grimace, as does my mother. Dad follows Grandma into the shed first. Approximately a dozen glass containers of various reptiles, mostly snakes, and, of course, live bait are scattered on shelving. Goose bumps implode as I try not to focus on all the slithering behind the cages. Grandma stomps back to a cage, lifting out the gray, thick and long serpentine. Big spots of bright gold on its slithery back keep it from camouflage. I flinch. Mom steps back, closing her eyes.

"Meet Sister Goldenhair!" says my grandmother.

"She's a beauty, Ma." Dad picks it up. "Python?"

Grandma nods. "Sweet as pie. Kathy brought her down for my birthday."

"I'm gonna check on Woolfie," I say.

Mom joins me as we hop outside to watch

the dog frolicking, or rather terrorizing the cats. We walk over to the pile of wood. "Can you believe she does all this herself?" I say to Mom.

"Your grandmother is one the most interesting and independent women I've ever met."

We tame Woofie down enough to make nice with a few of the cats. Grandma has finished her reptile presentation, inviting us in the trailer for a meal of grilled venison loin and roasted tomatoes from her garden. I see chocolate chip cookies on the counter awaiting us for dessert.

"Venison?" Mom asks. "I suppose you're gonna tell us you hunted the deer yourself."

Grandma shakes her head. "Wish I could. Alice got this one. We split the meat."

I eat as much venison as I can take, then sneak three of the cookies before collapsing on the couch.

"You better eat more of those cookies, little miss Ethiopia!" hollers my grandma.

She brings in a plate of cookies, so I grab three more. Mom looks to me with her eyes raised, and passes on the offer.

"None for me, Ruby," Mom says. "Moderation is my motto."

My family settles in around the small living quarters and soon we're discussing other extended family matters, with our usual splashes of drugs, unwanted pregnancies, and jail excursions. Then Grandma says, "Oh well. I'm a firm believer people find their way. Eventually. Most people anyway. Good people. I'm pretty sure our family is good people."

"Some people need more guidance than others," says my mother.

"Independent," Grandma says. "I raised my family to be independent. Who knows if that's right or wrong." Grandma turns to me. "So, your daddy says you're gonna be getting a masters in business?"

"I guess I am."

"And here I thought you were gonna teach music!" Grandma laughs. "Guess I'll have to tell Alice something different."

"Music?" Mom says. "It was never music. She had planned on going to law school, which I still think is not a bad idea–"

"Speaking of music," I say, "you should play guitar for us, Grandma!"

Grandma sighs. "I'm a little rusty, you know."

My dad pulls out a red acoustic Epiphone from behind Grandma's recliner. After she barely tunes the instrument, she begins to strum a few chords. And then she hums.

She's not rusty.

For the next hour, Grandma plays and sings us bits of country, blues, and hymns. She doesn't read any music, and her soft alto twang is like listening to the most perfect lullaby.

"Curt!" she demands. "Sing along with me."

Dad joins her for a verse of *Let the Circle Be Unbroken*, and I feel the untapped talent of my father's tenor voice reverberate throughout the tiny quarters.

"Can I sing with you?" I ask. "Something I know?"

We piece together a quiet tribute to *Amazing Grace*, with me in my pop soprano and Grandma in her country alto. My dad even ekes out a smile. "Amos can sing that one at my funeral," he says with a messing of my hair. Then with a sigh he adds, "We should get back on the road."

"Lemme speak to Amy for a minute." Grandma gets up, pulling me back to her bedroom which happens to be covered wall-to-wall with Jesus prints and crosses.

"I need to give you something," she says.

This is the moment I've been waiting for. A guitar. She's finally going to give me one of her guitars. Maybe the twelve string. I'm a total novice, but intend to tackle this instrument someday.

"Honey, you've never asked me for any money." She puts her hands on my shoulders and looks me in the eyes.

"I don't need money–"

"I want to do this for you. What does one year of college cost?"

"Grandma. I really don't need money for college. Creighton gave me a scholarship. And I have a full-time job."

Grandma shakes her head. "I don't even know what you're gonna do with that Masters thing, but it sure does sound important." She pulls my chin up. "I won't lie though. It seems to me that yer a musician, honey. But you gotta do what you think is right."

She continues to open a large jewelry box and pulls out a wad of hundred dollar bills. Apparently, Grandma doesn't believe in banks.

"Here's $3,000. It's not much, but I want to help you out somehow."

"Not much? I can't take that."

"I'll be pretty damn mad if you don't. Now, your grandpa is real proud of you. He tells me these things. In my dreams. He tells me these things."

I wrap my arms around her and kiss her wrinkle-stained cheek.

"How do I thank you?"

"Someday, pass your fortunes on. There'll come a day when you realize you don't need much to be happy."

As we return from our day trip to Rockport, I pet Woolfie whose head lays in my lap. I realize my heart has been lifted. And it has absolutely nothing to do with the wad of cash sitting in Mom's purse.

"She probably wanted to make sure she didn't have any money around to bail Carissa out of jail again," Dad says.

"Why would you say that?" Mom smacks Dad in the shoulder. "Don't you think that would hurt Amy's feelings?"

"Even so," I say. "She didn't have to give it to

me, Dad. I tried not to take it."

As we approach our house, I'm overcome with the desire to play the piano. Maybe God was sending me a message through Grandma. Play more music. It makes me happy.

I run to the music room and thumb through some sheet music. Bach. Both hands attempt to scamper on the keys, mimicking melodies in the treble and bass clefs to keep my mind completely engaged. It's been too long.

Left-hand! Come on, keep up with the runs. I stop to practice the bass clef at half the tempo and twice the volume.

"Amy!" Mom startles me with a spine-tingling shout.

"What?" I ask, a little peeved.

"Someone's here to see you." She stands in the doorway and points to the kitchen as if she's giving away the person with her gestures.

My stomach sinks as I think about Brad. Last week he told me he'd swing by sometime before he left for college. Now Mom has betrayed her only daughter and let him in. Worse yet, he heard me playing piano. I can't even fake illness. Or can I? I begin a coughing attack as I slowly make my way through the hallway. Then I stop before reaching the kitchen and try to wipe my eye make-up off on my T-shirt, to give me a pale-faced, sickly look. Here goes. One more cough before I face him. I head into the kitchen to greet my guest.

When I step into the kitchen and turn to face the person sitting at the table, I regret wiping off my mascara. Because it's not Brad.

CHAPTER 29

ICE CREAM MAN

AUGUST 1992

Nick wears a Royals baseball cap low over his eyes, and fidgets with his thumbs.

"Hello," I say swallowing hard.

"Are you sick?" Nick asks. "Maybe I should come back."

"Allergies," I lie. "Thanks for asking."

I position myself at the edge of the kitchen.

"I just came to wish you well. Before you left for the summer. And to say good luck."

Biting my lip, I give him the slightest of nods.

I avoid his eyes, unsure how to react. Woolfie taps across the kitchen floor to lap up some water. I'm relieved to have something to focus my eyes on besides Nick.

"Wanna get some ice cream?" he asks. "I'll buy."

I shift about, considering what to say when he adds, "If you don't want to, that's fine."

"Sure."

Could've done without all those cookies in Rockport today.

We ride to the Dairy Queen in silence. Once we arrive and he turns off the engine, he asks, "Are you leaving then?"

"I begin school in two weeks."

He nods, as if he knew the answer already. Turning to me, he says, "I'm really sorry. Hopefully, you understand. I just don't want to hold you back. But if you end up coming back here someday, I imagine I'll still be here." He takes a deep breath. "Maybe we could get together when you make it back here to visit. Or something. You know, like on your college breaks?" He pauses, waiting for a reaction. "Or not. I understand if you wouldn't want to."

"Nick, I need to tell you–"

"I totally understand. But you should know I really do like you. A lot. I can't stop thinking of you." Nick puts his head down. "When you walked out of the house that night, I felt so bad. It's been a horrible summer for stuff like that. I know it probably doesn't really matter now, but when when I saw you eating with Brad, I got so jealous. Crazy jealous. Maybe I should've been happy for Brad because he's my friend and all. But I wasn't. I wanted to be taking you to lunch."

I hold back my smile. "Nick, I never wanted

us to stop seeing each other." After a deep, steady breath I say, "I'm not leaving. Took the job. And I'm enrolled in the MBA program at Creighton. Sorry if that makes you mad."

Nick takes off his cap and rubs his head. "Mad? How can I be mad? You should be mad at me."

Like balloons being popped by a pin, tension begins to dissolve between us. He jumps out of the truck, poking his head through the open window. He pulls his cap back on and asks, "You want a sundae?"

I shake my head.

A gooey parfait?"

"I don't want anything."

"Nothing? Seriously? You take the fun out of ice cream."

After Nick leaves, I glance down at my shirt. A grungy Budweiser T-shirt. Lyn's endearing gift before she left for Chicago. Eye shadow smudged all over the corners. When did my wardrobe begin its descent?

Nick returns with two chocolate shakes – large enough for two small horses. Either he's gonna force the frozen treat on me, or he's really hungry.

"Hungry?" I ask him.

"I'm sorry I never told you congratulations," says Nick setting one of the shakes between his legs, "like a normal person, when you were accepted into that program."

He starts the truck and leaves the parking lot, expertly navigating the road and his desserts.

"Where are we going?" I ask as I see him headed in the opposite direction of my house.

"I'm ecstatic you decided to stay. But you gotta promise me something?"

"What?" I ask.

"When you start looking for a real job, don't let me influence your decision." I wrap my arms around myself as he continues. "You need to be happy in what you do before you can be happy with someone else."

I nod, wanting this discussion to be over.

Picking up the extra shake between his legs I ask, "Want me to hold your other shake?"

"It's not for me. Although..." He shows me his mostly-finished cup. "But I won't. It's for someone else. Someone I want you to meet."

"Who?"

He glances at me then puts his cup on the floor. "My brother. My older brother, Dave."

"You have a brother? And you didn't you tell me?"

He shrugs. "Didn't figure you'd be around long enough to bother."

Within a few quiet minutes, we pull into the Little Flower Haven nursing home. The name is deceiving. I only see generic shrubs around the place. No flowers.

I follow Nick, striding through a building of peach and blue floral walls. (Aha. Flowers.) As we tour the corridors, I become dispirited by the overwhelming thick air, reminding me both of a school lunchroom and a hospital. When a skeletal, white-haired figure leaning at the edge of a door pokes her head out to shout, "I'm here! I'm here!" something clicks in me. Poor lady. Poor residents. I feel angry with myself for being critical of the living quarters. I make a point to smile at anyone we pass by, even if their heads are stooped.

Eventually we reach an assembly room with an aviary, a piano, and a large TV. Nick takes my hand as we step past a few wheelchairs and card tables.

Then I see him. It startles me to see a man so closely resembling Nick sitting in a motorized wheelchair. He seems to be staring directly at us. While his buzzed hair is noticeably blonder, and his eyes sparkle a glacier blue, his facial features are unmistakeable. I could've picked him to be Nick's brother out of a line up of a hundred.

"Hey dude! Aren't your Cardinals playing?" Nick approaches his brother, who doesn't respond. Nick rubs his shoulder.

Nick holds up the shake. "Not gonna help your diet today."

Dave's right arm curls into his side, with his left arm positioned on the wheelchair controls. Shifting his head toward Nick, he says in measured syllables, "Very good. Thank you, Nicky."

Holding the straw to Dave's mouth, Nick helps Dave position the cup, then steps away. "You got this," Nick says. "Brought someone to meet you, bud. Her name is Amy."

Dave lifts his face toward me.

"Happy to meet you," I say, extending my hand. He stares at my extended fingers as he holds his shake. I've just made this awkward. So I pat him on the shoulder, which is also awkward.

Nick sets two chairs up for us, taking a seat aimed toward the TV. He's also confiscated a remote.

"See any baseball scores today? Like how bad the Royals got beat?"

Dave points his thumb down. "Did you play baseball today Nickie?"

"We won the county tournament last weekend, remember? Season is over for me."

I turn to Nick. "Congratulations. Sorry I missed it."

Nick shrugs.

"How-how come you missed it?" Dave asks me.

I smile at Dave, wondering what to tell him. "Nick forgot to tell me about it."

Dave shakes his head, then turns to his brother. "You shouldn't forget to tell Sarah important things."

"Sarah's gone. This is Amy."

Dave studies me. "Pretty."

I blush. I hope he's talking about me, and not Sarah.

"She ain't too bad." Nick looks askance at me while controlling the remote, flashing through channels – commentating on a number of them as well. Dave says little, but smiles at me when Nick makes a joke. An old man on the couch nearby snores and talks about Estelle, bringing us a few discreet laughs.

As soon as the old man on the couch awakens and decides to leave, I point to the piano in the corner.

"Want me to play something for you?" I look around the room. "Do you think they would mind?"

"Today was the first time I ever heard you play. I can't imagine they'd mind at all."

To impress my small audience, I start off with the first section of a Schubert sonata that is forever imprinted in my memory, full of impressive-sounding runs. It's actually easier than it sounds. Then I move on to a crowd-pleaser–Debussy's Clair de Lune.

As Nick applauds, he says to Dave, "A show-off, isn't she?"

"Perhaps you'd prefer something more contemporary?" I hammer out a medley of classics like Jackson Browne's *The Roadies* and Clapton's *Layla*. When I meld in the first few measures of *Home Sweet Home*, someone shouts out, "Motley Crue!" I stop playing to see a male nursing aide with a spiky haircut and an impressive dragon tattoo.

"Chad! Chad Hickerson," Nick shouts, walking over to greet the headbanger. "How you been?"

"Not bad. All cleaned up now. Working on getting my LPN. Trying to do something with my life."

"Good for you. Haven't seen you for awhile. Didn't even know you worked here."

"I overdosed! Got into some shit. Nasty stuff." Chad pulls out a wallet. "But I got a reason to live now, you know. Take a look at her."

"She's a cutie," Nick says. "How old? Two?"

I watch Nick and Chad talk, noticing how Nick is completely engaged in every detail of Chad's poor, distraught life – some guy I've never even heard about until two minutes ago. How could I *not* love this guy? He's such a good person. He's a freaking saint. A freaking, hot saint. Okay, maybe not a saint, but he's certainly a champion for the underdog. It's probably why he won't give up on the Royals.

After Chad leaves, Nick says we should go. He kneels before his brother and gives him a high five. Then he stands and hugs his head. "Love ya man."

"Yer embarrassing me," says Dave.

"Sorry to ruin your image," says Nick as he wraps his arms around me to go.

Taking Dave's hand I say, "I hope to see you soon."

"Thank you for coming," he says, looking me in the eye without blinking. "Would you mind taking me to my room first?"

"Not at all."

We take a leisurely walk back to Dave's room. Once again, I attempt eye contact with other residents in the hallway. I sense my attempts are in vain. But not always.

Once Dave is settled into his room, I notice a picture of a teenage girl amidst his family pictures. I ask Nick for the story as soon as we leave.

Nick explains when Dave was a senior in high school he was taking his girlfriend to a movie in Omaha on a rainy day–a day they couldn't harvest. On the way home, they were struck by a drunk driver who crashed straight into the passenger's side. His girlfriend was killed on impact. Dave barely made it. The doctors warned that if he survived, he would probably only be a vegetable. He progressed further than the doctors ever predicted.

"I'm surprised I don't remember the story. So tragic," I say.

"Dave was the star pitcher," Nick continues. "Was even being scouted by some of the colleges down south. But he wanted to stay close to home so he could come back and farm with Dad. Planned on going to University of Nebraska."

"Does he ever talk about his girlfriend?"

"Sometimes. He'll tear up. I try to keep him focused on baseball and farming. Mom gets him out there a couple of times during harvest. Being outside seems to perk him up."

"I can't believe you didn't tell me all this before."

"Like I said," he turns to me, feeling for my hand, "wasn't sure where we were headed. And Dave has some trouble remembering Sarah left me."

I'm not sure where we're headed either. And knitting myself into his family web probably isn't the best strategy for branching away.

CHAPTER 30
DOCTOR LOVE

SEPTEMBER 1992

Fourth week into the semester. Whole new world for me. My car and I have become quite intimate; although, I'm suspecting the tires are whispering about some vacation time. And guess what? I've gained, like ten pounds. Turning into a real fatty. The damn Mothers at the bank keep bringing all this freaking food. Amazing, delicious, fattening food. Scotcharoos. Almond bars. Ice cream desserts. So before my ass becomes a real problem, I'm considering a plan for myself. Perhaps rising at 4:30 to do aerobics with psychotic Denise Austin. It's an idea worth considering (if I actually follow through). And about all I can squeeze out, since the rest of my day is chock full of processing loans, fulfilling my assistantship duties for Professor Beaumont, or attending class.

Currently, I'm grading papers at McDonalds before my first class begins. (Okay, maybe McDonald's isn't the best choice for my new diet plan, but in my defense, I'm only eating the french fries.)

Life at Creighton is so different than my time in Iowa City. I was awestruck when I stepped on to the campus of the University of Iowa. Whether it was the sheer number of its 30,000 students scurrying about, or the Pentacrest with its colossal, historic buildings standing guard at the heart of the campus, I'm not sure. But I was swept up in the college spirit. Every day it seemed I was discovering new faces, different places, bizarre forms of art. The classrooms even amazed me, often hosting over five hundred students in one lecture room.

Now as I attend classes at this smaller, albeit quaint Creighton campus with the ornate St. John's Cathedral as its epicenter, my attitude is much more practical. My presence here at Creighton feels like an extension of my job. Classes are tasks to complete to elevate me into something I want to consider a "career." Although, I did happen to pass through a choir practicing the other day. My heart dropped about thirty feet. I hung around until the choir found the tears in my ducts. Then I scuttled away.

As I slurp the last of my mega Diet Coke, I eavesdrop on a conversation between two girls, presumably college students.

"I was so totally drunk! Do you really think Brock noticed me?"

"Totally. He was scamming on you all night, Elizabeth! The next Sigma Pi party is Friday night. We are going to crash it for sure. William's going to be there. He's so hot."

"Does William, like, know you're alive?"

Elizabeth's friend is quiet for a moment. I move in to listen for the response. It occurs to me this William could be Nick's infamous cousin. I wouldn't be surprised.

"You know, Elizabeth, you're not the only girl who gets noticed."

"I didn't say that I was, Tiff! I just didn't know you and William ever talked."

"We have Chemistry together. We talk occasionally in lab. He says he's pre-med."

I feel obliged to contribute to the conversation, so I turn in my booth and face the girls, who are both brunettes with heavy doses of Estee Lauder.

"Have either of you studied economics?" I ask.

They look at me blankly, eyebrows perched, as if I'm insane.

"Well, there's this theory of opportunity cost. It values the damage of lost opportunities when other alternatives present themselves."

The girls chew on their straws, watching me with a fair amount of suspicion.

"What I'm saying is that William could be your real deal. If you don't tell him how you feel, you might be losing out on love."

One of them looks to me. "How do you put a

value on that?"

"You'll wonder the rest of your life, won't you?"

When I slide back down into my booth, I hear them whisper. Maybe even giggle. Hopefully Tiff has some new found courage to find her true love in William. Or at least find out if her feelings are misdirected. Then I wonder. Have I just transformed myself into a modern day Emma? Putting my nose into other people's business, just as Jane Austen would have depicted? The only difference is my mind has been heavily influenced by my business studies. I'm using economics in the art of persuasion.

I've been thinking a lot lately about Penny and Jeff. My sense is that he's not the right guy for her. But I can't quite bring myself to broach the topic with her yet. She keeps showing me bridal magazines, so I fear the opportunity hasn't presented itself.

But I think it's coming.

CHAPTER 31
THE MARCH

OCTOBER 1992

Farming is dangerous business. Sometimes fatal. This had not really occurred to me. Until this week.

I never even met the Nick's Uncle Louis. But images consume me since Nick explained how a tractor tipped, rolling over on the poor man as he was hauling corn. That could've been Nick. When I badger him on how such a horrible accident could've been prevented, Nick just says, "Sometimes this stuff just happens."

We dash into St. Mary of Fatima's to attend the funeral, out of the damp, downpour of a rain. As soon as we're inside, I'm suddenly struck by the space before me – the vacuous ceiling and infinite spires at the alter.

"I forgot how pretty this church is," I whisper to Nick. "Haven't been here since I used to attend church with Shandy Wilson when we were little."

"This church?" Nick twists his face, as he wipes off the rain from his forehead. "It's nothing compared to St. Joe's."

I'd like to pitch some sort of commercial about our Methodist Church, but my parents haven't attended since my maternal grandmother died ten years ago. And I certainly don't remember being awestruck by its orange carpeting and purple felt "Jesus Loves You" wall hangings.

Another detail that hasn't escaped me is Nick. He looks dashing in his herringbone taupe suit. As a matter of fact, I don't think I've ever seen a man look better in a suit, and I see men in suits all the time.

We wait at the back of the church to meet up with the rest of his family. Off to our side is the grieving immediate family gathered around the big black casket. More people fill into the pews while organ music plays softly in the background. We are quiet as we watch the family hug and sniff back tears. Then from somewhere in the grieving circle, Helen and Joe emerge to join us. Straightening his tie, Helen starts to fuss over her son. "Nick, you look so handsome."

"I feel like a basketball coach," Nick says, pushing his mother away. Joe cracks a smile.

"The girls aren't here yet?" Helen asks impatiently. Within seconds of the statement, as if it were a command, both Judy and Jonie's families arrive. Jonie is miserable, trudging along as if she's just been defeated in a marathon. Her rotund stomach hardly looks real–a watermelon resides under her shirt.

"Mom, do we really have to march in?" asks Judy. "Jonie feels, and looks pretty awful."

"She'll be fine," Helen says. "All of the families should be ready soon."

I look at Nick questioningly, "Marching? As in the 'saints go marching in'?"

"Not quite New Orleans style." Nick responds with little explanation. As I look around, I notice the number of people packing in around us has doubled within the last several minutes, apparently for "The March."

Suddenly, a spry lady, about the same height as Helen, pops through a small opening in the crowd and announces, "There's that Klein clan."

"Aunt Mary Jane," Nick offers flatly.

"Hello, my little Nickie!" She turns to me, placing a hand on my cheek. "And how are you, Sarah? Any news of another grandbaby for Helen along the way?"

I look to Nick's family, who remain silent with smirky smiles. Not one of them steps in to introduce me. Not even Nick. So I play along.

"You never know," I say rubbing my belly, then watch Helen's face turn stony with my ill-timed attempt at humor.

"Don't wait too long. You don't want to be an old crotch chasing babies around." Then she faces

Jonie. "My. You are big. You sure there ain't twins in there?" Mary Jane edges her nose towards Jonie's bump, as if to inspect for twins. Jonie seems to stand taller, as if to challenge her aunt by taunting the womb in her face. If the plan was to repel, it worked. Mary Jane prances on to the next family.

"Mom's oldest sister. She's not just *a* royal pain in the ass, she's *the* royal pain in the ass."

For the next fifteen minutes, I'm presented a history of Helen's side of the family. Five sisters and three living brothers. Another brother killed in World War II. Five thousand cousins, spouses and children.

"Mary Pat..."

"Ann Mary..."

"Mary Grace..."

"Ellen Marie...."

I whisper to Nick, "What's up with all the Mary's and Marie's?"

He shrugs.

Helen overhears the comment. "What church were you baptized in?"

"United Methodist."

"How nice," says Judy. "Bet your middle name isn't Maria."

"Like both of ours," adds Jonie.

Family by family, we march to our seats. Finally, the funeral begins. I can't help but watch Uncle Louis' wife. She keeps her grave face level; although, it's apparent she either hasn't slept or is overwrought from crying. Probably both. Every family member around her is crying, while she passes around the tissues.

"She looks tired, but strong," I whisper to Nick.

"An act," he says. "Mom says she's pretty torn up. She just booked their first cruise ever. Finally convinced him to do some traveling."

As soon Nick tells me this, I feel my shoulders slump. He grabs my hand and says, "You sure you want to be with a farmer?"

"Shht!" whispers Helen.

Nick begins to pick at his nails. Of course I want to be with Nick. But I want to travel. And I don't want him to die. Does Nick have to farm?

I try to focus on the Mass and not be distracted. I'm brought back to the moment as the priest compares Uncle Louis's love for his children to Jesus's love for all. But I'm struck most when I hear the priest say, "Louis always said he had the best life. No regrets. His life had been full and with love."

Maybe he didn't care about the cruise, but I wonder if his wife did.

I don't understand the rituals. I don't know most of the prayers. But I'm experiencing a sense of spiritual awareness among the congregation as we sing. My eyes stay fixated on the statue of Jesus on the cross adorning the wall behind the alter. The pipe organ begins and the music presses on my heart. I've never heard the hymn, but I feel like it swell within me.

"Do not be afraid, I am with you.
I have called you each by name.
Come and Follow me,
I will bring you home;
I love you and you are mine."

A tear surprises me by trickling down my cheek. Nick grabs my hand. "You okay?"

I nod, wiping back my mascara. "I always cry at a good funeral."

As he wraps his arm around me, comforting me over his dead uncle whom I never knew, I consider how perhaps my role should be to support Nick. And here he is, wiping away my tears. My tears over what?

The idea of losing Nick?

Choosing a life on the farm?

As we step out of the church, the rain has settled to a pitter. The crowd scatters to their cars, but Nick stops to press his lips into my ear. "I wouldn't let a tractor tip over me. Especially knowing I had you."

I believe he does see me in his future.

CHAPTER 32

HARVEST MOON

OCTOBER 1992

"Doesn't get much better than this, does it?"

We're harvesting corn. Well, Nick is actually harvesting corn. I'm more of an observer—a cheerleader of sorts.

"You know what I decided today?" I say to the man in this cab, operating gears and levers as if he's flying a plane. "Autumn is the most charming time of the year."

"You just discovered this?" asks Nick. "Kind of a given, ain't it?"

I had intended to rant on about the beauty of the crimson and gold landscapes covering our county using the adjectives crimson and gold, then boast about the crispy evening weather...perfect for sweatshirts and sleeping with the window open. I was feeling all poetic. But judging by Nick's reaction, I'm feeling perhaps my reflections are common place. Perhaps I'm not so clever after all.

This October day has been unseasonably hot with insects bursting to life, chatting near my ears most of the day. But as the chill sneaks up, they finally start to grow lethargic. Nick's is too busy to notice anything else going on. I try not to shiver, focusing on the panoramic view, which is fairly astounding. A purplish sun makes its way west, exploding throughout the sky and setting its last rays on the fields, as if it's kissing the earth goodnight. Gosh. All these poetic phrases going to waste in my head. But Nick appears a bit occupied to appreciate my observations right now, especially about scenery.

Corn dust settles in my nostrils, giving me a sneezing convulsion, which has the perk of waking up my butt which has fallen asleep on the tiny buddy-seat.

"Gesundheit times ten," says Nick.

As soon as we hit a stretch of cruising altitude, he grabs my knees and asks, "You sure you want to be here? Love the company, but I'm sure you could find something more fun than this. Maybe go out with Penny?"

"Jeff only allows her out on our designated Thursdays," I say. "Controlling jerk. Can't figure out how such a confident girl would choose him."

Nick jumps up from his seat, pointing out the window. "Did you see that?"

"What?" I stand to look over the giant iron

cones, only to see them sweep up dry stalks. "What am I seeing?"

"Keep watching."

After a few hundred yards, I see it. A small, white leaping blur skitters before us.

"A dog!"

"It's a fox," says Nick. "A young one. Hardly ever see the white ones."

"Beautiful," I say, noticing the magnificent ears of the animal as it darts in and out of the rows. "Will it get out of the way for you?"

"Foxes are pretty quick," says Nick. "Although this one seems to be testing fate—"

And that's when we hear a thump. Something in the motor starts to grind into a terrible sound.

"Fuck." Nick shuts down the combine, and peeks over the edge. "Oh Christ. Don't look."

But that's exactly what I do. A bloody head of the little fox is wedged between the corn snouts. I scream, covering my face. Nick climbs out of the combine, while I remain still.

I wait in my seat, chin down, trying not to cry, listening to Nick curse as he does who-knows-what with the poor animal. Once he returns, he starts the engine and stares straight ahead. Finally I ask, "I don't suppose it could've been saved."

He doesn't say anything.

"Has that ever happened before?"

He shakes his head. "Not to me."

"I hardly ever see foxes around here. You'd

think Fox Plaine would be swarming with them," I say. "It was so cool. I mean before–"

"I don't feel so good," says Nick. "Can we not talk about this?"

He rubs his eyes, then looks at me with his face more pallid than I've ever seen. "I'm sorry. Take me some place else right now. I need to think about something else."

Oh no! Nick appears pukey. Think! Quickly! What would distract Nick?

"I've been thinking. There's this new sushi restaurant in Omaha we should try. Have you ever had sushi?"

"Please. Amy. Something not disgusting. You can't imagine what I just had to do."

And for once, I'm without words. Can't offer a single topic to this poor man. Maybe because I'm unbendingly stuck in the image of the fox as well.

So we sit in the combine for the next several minutes without speaking. Until I think of the most brilliant conversational piece ever.

"I called my friend Paul the other day."

After Nick's slight shift of a shoulder which I interpret as acknowledgement, I add, "Paul's the gay one. Apparently, he has a new love interest. Some student working on his MFA as well. Doing a thesis on Hemmingway and Fitzgerald."

"That stuff's beyond me."

"I find it just a bit ironic."

Nick shrugs. "I'm never gonna be able to talk

books with you."

"Never is a long time." I squeeze his arm. "Hey. I'm sitting in a combine. Never pictured myself doing that."

Nick points to a white pickup inching its way through the field.

"Nice. Mom's bringing supper out. I really have no appetite"

"So early?"

"Dad eats at 5:30 every night. It's their arrangement. If I don't eat with them, it's like I've committed a Cardinal sin." He sighs, banging his hands on the steering column. "So. I'm gonna shut off the engine, swallow the bile in the back of my throat, and eat maidrites and chips to avoid any confrontation. You are most welcome to join me."

We climb down this gigantic piece of machinery while Joe drives a tractor and wagon toward us. Nick turns to stomp through the stocks as I trail behind him, attempting to navigate the piercing corn stocks. Then he stops and turns around.

"This isn't the life for everyone," he says. "Not every wife wants to bring supper out to their husband."

"I bet not. Not everyone can make a sloppy joe. And God forbid if you figure out how to pack a lunch for yourself."

Dropping his head, he starts picking at his fingernails. "I'm sorry." He looks up. "Why am I doing this to you? There's no reason." Then he shuffles through a row to wrap his arms around me. "Harvest isn't usually so gory. I really do want to enjoy every minute I get to spend with you."

I don't find comfort in his words, nor the way he holds me so tightly, as if he's afraid to let go.

CHAPTER 33
THANK YOU

NOVEMBER 28, 1992

Pumpkin Butter Pecan Dessert.

The Loam County Fair's Blue Ribbon Cookbook has this recipe classified as "three apples." An indicator of difficulty–the highest difficulty in fact. But I'm undaunted. It's time for me to prove my cooking abilities to Nick. To the world. After all, I'm smart. I'm a native of this county. And I want to bring a fabulous dish to the Klein family Thanksgiving.

"The kitchen's all yours," says Mom as she bastes the turkey over the oven. Sage and poultry juices waft throughout our house this early morning as I shift into pastry chef. Mom seals up her bird, then looks over my shoulder at my project. "What time are you headed to the Klein's today?" she asks.

"Late this afternoon," I say rubbing my temples.

"You sure about that particular dessert?" she asks. "Looks complicated for novices."

I take my cookbook to the other side of the kitchen. And begin.

It's been two hours since Mom left me and my ambition. Now she worms her way back into the kitchen to witness my ambition twitter into anxiety. Inspecting the nuts in the bottom of my pan, she says, "You know you could've bought the pecans pre-chopped."

"No way," I say. "Well. Chopping pecans was a nice way to ramp up the arthritis in my hands. Very therapeutic."

Focused on my second layer, I whip and whip and whip, hoping this batch of cream cheese and sugar will take the form of something like pudding any day now.

"Mom?" I ask, suddenly in need of a matriarch. "Do you think this looks soupy or creamy?"

"Did you happen to use low fat cream cheese?"

"Saving on calories."

I assume she'll appreciate this, but she twists her face. "Ooh. Not good for desserts."

"It's suppose to chill," I say. "It should set then, right?"

"Maybe."

As I pour my top layer over the nutty crust, the creation doesn't quite present itself as I'd hoped.

Still, I'm confident the chilling will help–along with my pumpkin whip cream mixture I have set aside. I don't think I've messed this part of the recipe up.

Mom tastes the whippy pumpkin. "This tastes good."

I take the bowl from her to pour my final layer. And as I do, the mixture heaves over the pan in clumps. The dessert now resembles baby puke. I look to my mom. She comes over with a spatula and begins to spread the pumpkin as if she's buttering toast. Then she takes a container of Cool Whip to frost my concoction.

"Good move Mom!" I say, while giving her a hug. "You've made it palatable. In appearance at least. Now. Let this chill and I'm off for a fifteen minute nap. Late night."

Sneaking off to the living room, I collapse on the sofa.

Guilt-ridden thoughts from last night keep me from completely dosing off. The party at The Foxy had to be one of the more celebrated drunk fests of the year, with so many returning home for the holiday. With all the people around, what in the world induced me to introduce my cousin to Will? One of the most unabashed chauvinists I know?

Damn tequila.

"Six months!" Carissa said, tartly puffing on her cigarette. "Been clean for six months now. And I got this job at the sale barn."

White-trash pretty. In her bright magenta t-shirt, tied up to reveal her concave belly and big boobs. I couldn't even stop staring at her as she clipped around in her skintight jeans and high heels. Nick asked me why I didn't dress more like that.

Was if my fault that Will showed up at my side? Just as I asked Carissa if she was dating anyone? Maybe it was inevitable. Maybe they would've found each other anyway.

Mom shakes me from my thoughts, pulling me up from the sofa, away from last night.

"Kitchen duty. Now. Please."

After I finish cleaning up my mess, Mom starts to question me. "I assume you saw some of your old classmates last night. How are they? Shandy? Lyn?"

She knows how I feel about Shandy.

"Can I help you with the potatoes?" I ask.

She points to the scrubber, while getting the peeler out.

"Well," I say returning to her question while scrubbing a potato under the water. "Lyn is doing awesome. She's transferring to the University of Illinois in Urbana. Wants to get into their vet school."

Mom digs her peeler into the skin of a washed tuber, scraping with a certain measured cadence. "Now. That is something. Going to be a doctor. Dr. Axland. Isn't that just great...She's really making something of herself isn't she?" After a few quiet moments, she whispers, "A doctor. Hm."

After scrubbing another potato under the

cold water I say, "She loves animals. Lyn is passionate about animals."

Mom nods. And keeps peeling. After a considerable pause she asks, "Have you ever toured the law school at Creighton? I still think you might regret not considering it."

I have considered it, Mother.

After helping to finish the potato job, I leave the kitchen, mentioning a jog under my breath. I don't care if she hears me or not.

Once I step outside, the cold stings my eyes, making me shiver. Perhaps in another mood, I might change my mind about the idea of a jog. But not now.

My walkman, set to play U2's *Mysterious Ways*, assists to free me of my mother's disappointed inferences with its funky guitar, upbeat percussion, and Bono's sensual voice.

Lucky for me, my mind is back to Nick.

I wonder if Nick finds me mysterious. Should I try to be more demure? Exotic? Trashy like my cousin? So he doesn't grow bored with me? I wonder how often his ex-wife wanders into his mind. Maybe I should take extra measures to ensure banking fashion doesn't rub off on me. Not terribly sexy.

As I'm considering how to transform my no-nonsense style into something sleek, glamorous, and graceful, I suddenly trip on a buckled sidewalk. I fly through the air–somersaulting–before landing on my back in someone's ungiving yard of dead autumn grass. I peek up, relieved to find no one around.

Until a voice calls from the street.

"Are you okay?"

I roll my head to see a family getting out of a Chevy Citation, dishes in hand, seemingly ready to begin Thanksgiving activities.

I quickly bolster myself up. "Fine! Just enjoying the sky."

"Amy?" says the voice. "Amy Gaer?"

I turn to see a woman with long, straight hair, decisively parted. She sports round, wire-rimmed glasses. Mrs. Washburn. My vocal teacher.

I glance down to see blood trickling down my leg. How I injured my knee, I do not know. Wasn't I airborne?

"That looks awful," she says as her family stands as statues. "Come on inside."

She passes her dish to her husband, as she checks my knee. Her two small girls are standing behind their father, with stocking caps and double-breasted winter coats. Their eyes are wide, as they continue to stare. The throbbing has caught up to my humiliation.

"It's nothing. Really." I attempt to choke out a few brave-footed words, as my old teacher pulls me inside a cottage-like house.

"Happy Thanksgiving!" offers a small, leathery-faced man at the door. The house smells strongly of something other than roasted poultry.

Warm, sweet, and meaty. My mouth waters.

The children chime around their grandpa, I presume, as Mrs. Washburn's husband explains how we have an injured jogger in need of help, making me feel ridiculous.

After Mrs. Washburn takes me to a tiny bathroom with a rust-stained ivory pedestal sink, she asks, "So Amy. How in the world have you been? In law school by now?"

The last time I saw my vocal teacher was at my graduation party. She gazes at me, blinking through her smudged glasses, with part of a smile on her lips. I'm struck by the concern in her voice as she begins to clean up my wound.

Tears form.

"Oh," she says.

"I'm sorry. My knee just hurts."

Quickly I ramble on about how great I'm actually doing, working on my MBA and dating a local farmer.

She nods her head and smiles.

"You were always one of my favorite students."

"You probably say that to everyone."

"I do," she says. "Makes people feel good.

This makes me giggle.

Taking my hand, she leads me out of the bathroom into a crowded dining room with a table that barely fits in the space. Against one wall sets an old upright piano with a plethora of sheet music and piano books strewn about it. The rest of Mrs. Washburn's family crowds themselves in an adjoining living room, zoned on the television watching something like a parade. She settles into the bench.

"How well do you remember lyrics?" she asks.

I nod with a grin. This is one area of my life I should be considered a genius. I hardly ever need the Karaoke machine, actually. I do not forget lyrics.

"Kids!" she shouts. "Come!"

Pointing to me with her right hand, then with her left, she takes on the bass clef and plays a D, F sharp, and an A. I'm committed. I am now Rizzo, and I'm on the stage of Grease. *There are worse things I could do.*

When I have finished my ballad, the intimate audience claps and hoots for me, forcing me to curtsy.

"Sorry," I say. "Probably not a very Thanksgiving-like song."

"Show-tunes are our favorite around here," says Mr. Washburn.

"Do you have any place to go for lunch?" asks the old man. "We got plenty-a food. We won't eat this whole ham."

I look at the two little girls who are now twinkling some notes on the piano.

"Thanks for the offer, but I should probably get home to my parents."

Mrs. Washburn walks me to the door.

"You were a great Rizzo. Stole the show, really."

I turn to her. "To tell you the truth. I was really mad about not getting Sandy."

She nods. "I know. But I always figured you'd realize Rizzo was much more interesting than Sandy. And someday you'd thank me for it."

Her words pierce more than the chill breeze whipping around me. Did I ever thank Mrs. Washburn for anything in high school? She spent an enormous amount of time coaching me for contests, concerts, and all-state. All I ever thought about was not getting the lead in Grease.

"You were an amazing teacher," I say.

"It's easy to teach kids with incredible talent, Amy," she says. "Good luck with your MBA." She pats my shoulder and turns back inside.

As she recedes back into the comfort of her family, I consider the life she leads, surrounded by music all the time influencing kids with her own talent and passion. A morsel of regret seeps in. Teaching has never been a consideration for me. I've always wanted the stage. But now, seeing Mrs. Washburn makes me wonder. Should I have become a music teacher?

I plod away, contemplating the possibility, when the sight of the worn-out Citation makes me halt.

No. I don't think a teacher role would suit me, or my mother, very well.

CHAPTER 34

WHAT A NIGHT

NOVEMBER 28, 1992

I'm holding my dessert in my lap, which has barely been touched. It would've been nice to know about the predominant Klein nut allergy. Or so they said. Those who dared to try my dish made comments like, "interesting" or "that's kind of different." My dessert had to be eaten in a bowl...with a spoon...so it wouldn't run off the plate.

"Does your Dad like me?" I ask as Nick drives me home.

"Sure."

"I'm not so sure."

"Just because you and Dad aren't on the same page on issues doesn't mean he doesn't like you," he says. "Maybe just avoid bringing up any topics that might be considered controversial. Like Rodney King. Or interracial marriages."

"I can't believe anyone, in this day and age,

feels there's anything wrong with interracial marriages. I wasn't kidding when I said Mom always hoped I'd bring BJ Armstrong home from Iowa City."

"I wouldn't mind if you'd bring BJ home," Nick says. "That'd be awesome! I could show him a thing or two on the basketball court." Nick grabs my hand. "Don't worry about Dad. They're conservative. Old-fashioned. They don't see themselves as prejudiced. When they say stuff like that, my sisters and I just sort of smile to ourselves."

"Do you think it bothers them that I'm not Catholic?"

"Definitely." Nick looks askance at me.

"Really?" I let go of his hand and cross my arms.

"Who cares! Jim and Mike aren't Catholic either."

"I just want your family to like me. Is that so wrong?" I think back over the evening and the more angrier I begin to feel about things. "By the way, I can't believe how much your mom waits on your dad. Your dad didn't *ask* her. He *commanded* her! You don't think that's right do you?"

Despite my promise not to let my feelings sway my future, thoughts of marriage to Nick have this habit of creeping into mind. But I will not be enslaved to him.

"Probably not. But Mom wouldn't do it if she didn't want to. She's strong-willed too. I don't think it's wrong to do favors for each other, do you?" He looks to me. "Like, hey honey, would you grab me a beer while you're in there?"

"Well, no. But there's a difference between 'would you mind grabbing me a beer' and 'grab me a beer'."

"Oh, I see. It's approach we're talking about."

"Approach that means the difference between respect and condescension."

"Well, thanks for the clarification. I'll keep it in mind. But I do want to point out, my dad does respect my mom," he says with his head tilted. "You might be over-thinking it. Mom's not bitter."

That's what he thinks. But how can he be sure? Or, am I being bitchy about this? People should help each other out, I guess, right?

I'm sitting here feeling like this radical feminist, ready to burn my bra. But gosh, I'm not really like that. Or am I?

He grabs my hand again.

"By the way, they all like you. Sometimes you worry too much about stuff."

I nod my head. Next time, I will ask Nick to bring a three apple dessert.

And I'll just sing for the family.

CHAPTER 35

THE MOST WONDERFUL TIME OF THE YEAR

DECEMBER 1992

"Relieved finals are over?" Nick asks. "Or do you really love Christmas shopping this much?"

"I really love shopping this much."

The mall sheds silvery garland while boasting monstrous tree ornaments, strung about everywhere except on trees. People bustle all around, shuffling their bags and children through the claustrophobia of the crowd. Camping on to the mall's Christmas music ringing through the corridors, I sing, "*It's the Most Wonderful Time of the Year!*" A bald guy near me claps. I look to Nick who's now rubbing his eyes, his hands nearly covering his face.

"Embarrassed of me?" I ask.

"Not usually."

"Sorry, but not really." Nothing puts me in a better mood than Christmas shopping. "It's the holiday!"

"I just don't get into the whole gift thing. Or singing Christmas carols."

"You don't like giving gifts? Isn't that the whole point of Christmas, Mr. Catholic schoolboy?"

Nick pulls me through some paralyzed shoppers to a bench. I scoot closer to him, avoiding a spot of sticky, spilled hot chocolate.

"I have this history of buying the wrong gift," he says. "Clueless."

"Strange. And you even grew up with sisters." Nick examines his hands, ready to pick at his nails. "Let me help you out this year. I love buying gifts for people. Especially if it's not my own money."

His pensive, somewhat tortured expression doesn't flinch.

"I have an idea," I say grabbing his arm. "Let's make it easy. No gifts to each other."

"You don't really mean that," he says putting his knuckles to his cheeks. "Girls never mean that."

I'm trying to be the cool girlfriend.

"I mean it! Christmas should be for kids. Focus on your nephews."

Nick smiles over at me, with a seemingly whole new level of admiration for me. Perhaps I've just stepped up a notch in his book. Selfless, Jesus-like.

As we begin our journey again, Nick steps lighter. His face has brightened. Of course, I have stopped singing.

We pass a Zale's jewelry store. I try to steal a glimpse of Nick's profile to see if it's even on his radar. One minute ago, I said "no Christmas gifts," but I wonder if he'd consider any particular type of jewelry for me? Of the "engaging" type.

Ridiculous.

Nick proposing to me after only seven months of dating and only nine months after his wife left him. And who knows where my career will take me? Still, my sideward glance remains fixed on that store, in my extreme peripheral vision.

After an afternoon of shopping, we have a few heavy bags filled with toy tractors, baseballs, baseball hats, and baseball jerseys.

We decide to finish our shopping trip at the bookstore, to search for "dad" gifts, which of course delights me. As I'm feeling like a kid walking into a candy store, Nick halts abruptly. I scope out the scene, thinking I'm about to witness a robbery. But I only see a pregnant woman standing at the checkout counter.

She turns to face us.

Sarah. Nick's ex-wife. My eyes drop to her very pregnant belly.

As she steps toward us, I feel my face flush. (Too much candy. Wool scarf. Pregnant ex-wife.) Her confident stride is completely unnerving me.

"Hello, Nick." She looks to me, but rejects the idea of a greeting. I timidly offer a hello anyway.

Nick says nothing, staring at Sarah intently.

Seconds beat on and on while people slither around us. No one says anything. Finally she breaks the silence. "I hope you both have a nice Christmas." She brushes by Nick, rubbing against his shoulder. Nick grabs her arm as she almost passes him by.

Nick asks bluntly, "How far along are you, Sarah?"

Sarah smiles at him, almost flirtatiously and says, "I guess it's nothing for you to worry about anymore." Removing his hand, she begins to clip away in heeled boots. She's fairly graceful for being so pregnant. As we are both watching her, she stops and swivels around. "Happy New Year. Or did I say that already?" Then she edges her way back to grab Nick's hand.

"You look good, Nickie."

She tilts her head and almost says something else. But then walks away.

CHAPTER 36

I WANT TO GET AWAY

DECEMBER 1992

"Fly out to Chicago and stay with me for a while. It'll take your mind off the situation."

"Not a bad idea," I say to Jean as I squeeze my head together. "Would it seem like I'm deserting him?"

"You're not married to him. And why does he need you around for a paternity test?"

You're making way too much sense. I'm just afraid of losing him.

"Come out the weekend after Christmas and stay through New Year's. I'm invited to a party on the Navy Pier. Supposed to be an awesome band. Fireworks."

"You want me to be your date?"

"You'd be a great date. Maybe the best I'd had in a while."

"Sad."

"Most of the guys I've met seem to remind me of you. For some weird reason. Maybe it's because they read so much. If I believed in any of that superstitious crap, I'd say it's a sign you should come."

Jean knows how to lure me. Part of me wants to stay to keep Sarah from getting into Nick's head. But I sense a need to be absent as well. Chicago seems to be the answer.

"Okay. I'm coming."

Nick's Journal

December 13, 1991

She lost the baby.

Trying my best to console her.

We will try again. We need this baby. I think it might be the key to saving our marriage.

CHAPTER 37
NO APOLOGY

DECEMBER 1992

"Wanna go for a drive?" Nick asks, standing at my front door, rubbing his hands together as if he's nervous. "We should talk."

We've barely talked the last couple of weeks. I'm ready for it. I'm tired of staring out the window, wondering.

I nod.

"Where are you taking me?"

"Just driving," Nick says absently. But his steering feels defined. And I know this path. We're headed to Perling.

As we pass through the countryside, I announce my Chicago plans and how I just booked the flight yesterday.

"So I won't see you on New Year's?" he asks, tapping his fingers on the steering wheel. "Bummer.

But Chicago will probably be more fun than Fox Plaine. Gonna see Lyn as well?"

I knew it. He doesn't even care. His supportive attitude annoys me.

"I *knew* you wouldn't mind," I say, trying not to be cross.

"Of course, I mind." He glances at me. "But I understand."

"Look Nick. I'm not sure what's going on. We haven't exactly been talking."

He turns on the radio. Journey's *Don't Stop Believin* blares.

"We haven't, have we?" he says. Glancing at me, he adds. "Want to show you something."

Shivering on this blustering cold day, I consider what his show-and tell might be. Of course. A picture of the ultrasound. He's going to show me a picture of his baby just before he breaks up with me. We drive in silence, only hearing the guzzle of his Ford when we pull into the lane of his house.

"Just tell me. I can't stand it anymore."

"Almost here," he says.

Hiding my face into my mittens, I prepare myself. No crying. No crying.

"Hey!" he says, rubbing my back. "There's nothing to cry about."

I bolt up.

"Positive," he says with a smile.

As I look up, a hulking, black dog comes galloping toward us.

"Oh!" I say. "You got...a Lab?"

"Something like that," Nick replies with eyes flickering of pride.

No sooner than I slide out of the car, I'm welcomed with a clobber of snowy, grimy paws.

"Molly!" shouts Nick. "Behave."

I kneel in attempt to settle a happy dog who straightaway decides to scamper to Nick, lest she appear rude. Folding his arms around the canine's neck, Nick looks up at me to say, "I got her back."

"So are you going to be a father?" I ask.

"Sort of," he says, pointing to the dog as the wind begins whip around us. "Turns out, Sarah's not due until March. There's no way it could've been me. But she gave me the dog back. Pretty nice, heh?"

Relief! Happiness! Even a tint of jealousy streaks through me. Nick's not the father. But when did he meet up with his ex to get the dog?

"As a matter of fact, I found out her boyfriend already insisted on taking a paternity test."

It's time to douse my jealousy. I'm so tired of feeling this pit in my stomach when all I want to do is trust in this love I feel. Stepping toward Nick and Molly, I shout over the wind, "Merry Christmas!" Kissing Nick on the cheek, I whisper, "That's the best gift you could have given me."

"The best gift I could give you? That I'm not the father of another woman's child?"

Molly bounces up to check me on the cheek.

"I'm so easy–"

Nick pushes Molly away, pulling me into him. "Beyond adorable. Especially with your nose all Rudolph."

"I don't even feel cold."

The snow from the trees stirs around us as our bodies circle around each other. The small scale blizzard is inconsequential. I want to linger in this very moment for once, not considering my future nor my past, just the now.

Oh my God. I am so in love.

CHAPTER 38

JOY TO THE WORLD

DECEMBER 24, 1992

Sometimes mirrors are too candid.

All I can think is ridiculous. A hooker perhaps. Trying to pick up an elf. This pencil skirt and heels hardly atone for the fact I'm wearing an olive cable-knit poinsettia sweater. But the shirt came in fresh from Grandma so I'm compelled to oblige her. I ditch the skirt and heels for my stirrup pants and flats so it doesn't look like I'm trying so hard. But I begin to rush–Nick has been waiting here for fifteen minutes. Why *is* he so early? Church doesn't begin until 5:30. Clock reads 4:32.

Maybe he's excited about something tonight.

Maybe he's going to spring a surprise on me!

Would it be so horrible for me to change my career plans because of the love of my life?

I make my way through the house, hearing Mom and Grandma Ruby discussing exhaustive details of the food for tomorrow's Christmas celebration. Three different soups. Roast beef and ham. An extraordinary amount of bacon-wrapped appetizers. Mimosas. Sufficient dessert offerings to induce a diabetic coma. You'd think fifty guests were coming. But no. Just us and my aunt and uncle. Possibly Carissa. It's like this every year. We'll eat leftovers for weeks. Until we spot mold.

"Look alright?" I ask Nick who's watching *A Christmas Story* with my dad and Woolfie who has become the laziest dog ever. Or he just really loves TV with my dad.

Rising quickly, he tilts his head, then nods half-heartedly.

"Not dressy enough?" I ask, worried by his reluctant response. Maybe he's put off by the poinsettia.

"It's fine," he says. "We need to go." Suddenly I feel self-conscious about my choice of clothing.

"Mass starts at 5:30, right?" I ask.

"Yeah." He begins to usher me out. "We better move."

As we drive to St. Joseph's Catholic Church in Perling, snowflakes flutter in the headlights of the dark night. I crack the window to allow the cold air to filter in.

"Any reason you need the window open?"

"To smell the fresh snow!"

"Okay?"

"This is the kind of snowfall that makes you love where we live."

"Sorry. Don't concur. Snowfall does not make me love where we live," says Nick, but I'm sensing a certain sparkle through his scowl.

I shut the window and sigh. "Maybe I'm just nervous for your family celebration tonight. The cool air felt good to me." I face Nick. "Your Mom told me not to bring any food."

"Awesome," Nick says. "I mean, less work for you."

I nod in agreement, not completely offended. Finals were way more important to me than figuring out what dish to bring.

"Hey, cue me when to kneel and stand tonight in church," I say jabbing him in the shoulder. "I didn't do so well at your uncle's funeral."

"I noticed."

"You're not helping my anxiety."

"Just remember, going to church isn't about looking good or performing the right actions–"

"I know," I say, feeling a bit shallow.

"It's about taking a bulletin. Proving to your parents you went to church."

His parents do query him a lot on his church attendance.

We arrive in Perling and make our way to the top of the hill where St. Joseph's is perched with its towering steeple overlooking the town. I understand now why Nick wanted to leave so early. For such a small town, scores of people in their puffy coats and dress clothes are assembling lines as if a sold-out concert is about to begin.

Nick guides me up the steps to the tall oak arched entrance. As he holds open the creaky door, the pipe organ hums with a magnificent resonance. Illuminated mainly from white lights and candles, intricately-painted statues of saints guard the walls. I'm reminded of a Renaissance painting. Children belt out *Away in the Manager*, with one particular voice singing most wonderfully off-key.

We sneak into a small spot, squeezing into a pew near the back.

"Pretty church," I whisper to Nick.

"The prettiest." He points to the balcony to see the children's choir. "Maybe you could audition."

The Mass is in full swing as I study the church, which was obviously designed to have grand weddings. I bet all starry-eyed girlfriends get sucked into that dream when they walk in here. Scanning this large house of worship, I imagine where a trendy bride and most handsome groom would stand. Then, as my dream grows a bit boring, not thinking beyond a wedding ceremony, I find myself counting the spires on the walls behind the altar. My eyes lead me to a cove of three women statues. Presumably in the center is Mary, since she's holding a baby. Her gown bedazzles in royal blue, but she wears a modest bed sheet for a head scarf. The woman to the left of Mary wears a light blue, loosely-draping frock, set off by a nun's habit. Totally unassuming. The woman to Mary's right seems just a touch ostentatious with a flattering brown sheath, accented by a sage green robe, pulled together perfectly by a gold belt–each piece fitted to flatter the lady's figure. She even has the audacity to wear a crown. With all these meticulously-adorned statues, a bride and her bridesmaids will definitely need to go elaborate.

Suddenly, I'm brought back into the service when the priest orates about "sharing our gifts" with each other. While I completely understand the message has nothing to do with material goods, my mind quickly considers the possibility of whether Nick got me a gift, despite our little pact. Actually, not just *a gift–the gift* of all gifts. I look to him and smile. He smiles back.

After an hour and a half, the choir is singing *Joy to the World* while the priest and the alter boys march out of the church. As Nick and I exit, we are "Merry Christmas'd" by just about everyone who attended Mass. Spreading this joy feels so happy with all the pink-faced smiles and stranger-pats on the shoulders, I'm almost teary-eyed. But I hold back. I don't want Nick to see me crying in church again.

After we leave, Nick turns to me and says, "Before we go to my parents, we need make a stop at my house."

Oh my gosh. This is it.

We drive back to his house, and my heart is pounding canon balls.

"Should we listen to some music?" I ask, wanting to disguise the beating of my heart.

"Sure."

Rockin' Around the Christmas Tree.

A song so cornball, it parodies itself. But suddenly I find myself singing it with utter happiness.

Pulling into Nick's driveway, I make the confession before he has a chance to make any major scene.

"I hope you're not too upset, but I got you a gift."

"Shocking!" He turns off his engine. "My little Christmas elf got me something. It fits in your purse, huh? Good. Because my gift to you is really–."

"Small?" I dig around my small clutch to offer him a small box. "Small is good."

"Should we go inside?" he asks. "Open gifts by the tree?"

After we scurry inside and Nick plugs in his tree (decorated with a string of lights and one strand of garland), I insist on him opening my gift. He seems very appreciative of the four pairs of Creighton basketball tickets.

"Take whomever you want," I add. "It doesn't have to be me."

"Who else would I take?"

Now I hold my breath as he pulls out two gifts–much bigger than the size of a ring box. I let my breath out as I force a smile.

"You won't hurt my feelings if you don't like

either of these. Return 'em if you want."

"I wouldn't do that."

"You might."

I open the first shirt box to find a large olive cable-knit sweater with a large poinsettia. The sweater I'm wearing. Only bigger.

"It's cute," I remark holding it up. "Just my style."

"Mom says you shouldn't wear sweaters that fit too tight."

"Gosh no."

I hug Nick, whispering thank you in his ear. Then I step away to put the sweater on over my other sweater, which fits more like a dress. He hands me my other gift which I tear apart. A book on astronomy with a guide to mythological references.

"A book?" I read the description. *Astronomy and Mythology.* I'm immediately enchanted by the idea of a reference guide for one of my mild fascinations.

"I see you staring at stars all the time," Nick says. "I assume you're making lots of wishes." Taking my hand he says, "Hope you get everything you wish for."

As if I'm gazing into the night sky, I lock into his eyes. Then I fold into him, just before I make my Christmas wish.

Somehow, some way, our future together will miraculously align.

CHAPTER 39
CHICAGO

DECEMBER 1992

I have to admit, I really like this city.

And truth be known, I wish to be the one wearing a royal blue pea coat, like my stylish friend on this sunny, yet polar-infused, afternoon. Instead I sigh at my generic-labeled windbreaker as Jean and I make our way through the crisp air of Michigan Avenue, having plundered through an impressive number of stores already. She carries shopping bags from Marshall Fields, Crate and Barrel, Saks Fifth Avenue, Gap, Niketown, and Nordstrom's. My load is a bit lighter–an oversized Gap sack which holds an "After Christmas-Sale" sweater. Oh, and a half-eaten bag of multi-colored M&M's from the candy store.

"Wanna grab lunch?" Jean asks me. "At the new bookstore?"

I have died and gone to a bibliophile's heaven

as we dine in the store's bistro. Biting into into a juicy chicken salad sandwich, I try to not to swallow the food whole. But I'm anxious. My eyes dart around the bright three-story building abounding with books. People are roving with their noses positioned low, inspecting every nook and cranny of this store, ensuring no book has been left undiscovered. My foot begins to tap.

"You must love it. Living here. I can't imagine a Borders in Fox Plaine. Unless, of course, it had a bar."

"That's not a bad idea, really."

"You know I've always envied you," I say after shoving down my last bite. "And now this."

"Now what?"

"Look!" I say pointing around me.

"I have Borders?"

"Chicago. Culture. We've done so much already. The Chicago Art Museum. A Bulls game. And tonight we're going to a party on The Navy Pier! Do you think I'll be sophisticated enough for your work friends?" I glance down at the chicken salad that just dropped on my jacket.

Jean smiles, but I notice her eyes go vacant.

"I do like it here," she says while stirring her lettuce around.

"You don't sound convincing. What else do you want?"

"Nothing," she says, digging into her salad. "What else could I possibly want."

Jean is lonely. I just realize this.

I ask, "Have you made friends here?"

"Oh yeah. From work. They tend to be married or engaged." The speed of her mastication is slower than mine, and her chewing is intense, almost ponderous. I wait for her to swallow. She'd never talk with her mouth full. "Work keeps me busy."

I don't have a crumb left on my plate, while Jean's salad looks almost entirely untouched. Has Loam County turned me into a pig?

"I'm having fun now," Jean says. "It's been great having you here. It's especially nice not having to clean up your puke." She puts her fork down to face me. "So once you get your MBA, what are you going to do? Have you thought about where you want to live?"

"I think about it all the time," I say, rubbing my hands together, in attempt to remove the chicken salad goo. "I don't have it figured out."

"Come join me," she says with a twinkle in her eye. "I think I could handle you as a roommate again."

I put both of my hands on my cheeks, slamming my elbows on the table. "I will definitely keep it in mind."

"You don't seem so excited by the invitation."

I grab my fork and start picking at Jean's salad to help her out. "You must know I haven't minded living at home lately. Finding a new appreciation for my Fox Plaine."

"Oh my gosh." She pauses. "Are you really that much in love?"

I try not to pick at the food in my teeth since I'm in Chicago, but there seems to be a whole piece of lettuce wedged between my two front choppers. Once I'm reasonably assured the culprit is removed, I jump up. "If you're gonna take three hours to finish that salad, I'm gonna browse for books."

Holding up a finger, she says, "Hey, find me more Dickenson, would you?"

"Really?"

She nods. "I'm stepping from 'plank to plank.'"

I give her a broad smile. "You and me both, sister."

I curve my way to the fiction area, taking a glance at the area of new releases. Anne Rice. John Grisham. Stephen King. Madonna. Madonna? I decide to pass on her literary take of Sex and turn to the dedicated fiction aisle.

How's one to begin to tap all these books? Perhaps by starting with the letter A. My eyes zero in on Margaret Atwood.

"Dystopian fan?" asks a guy with preppy, tortoise glasses and a dark red scarf, as if he just got kicked out of lecture hall for trying to imitate a professor. He sips on his coffee, but doesn't move his eyes from the section of books before me.

I put my head down, thumbing through pages of *The Handmaid's Tale* and shrug. "Not particularly."

"I'm always pulled in by a well-designed book

cover as well," he says. "But that book is thought pro-voking, for sure."

I return the book, smile politely, and move past my uninvited recommender, on to the Cs. I find myself staring at the small cache of Tom Clancy novels, wondering if a spy thriller would spark Nick's interest in reading.

"So, you like espionage plots," says the guy, stepping to the other side of me. "Read *The Pelican Brief* yet?"

I shake my head. "Just looking at books for a friend." I pull out *The Hunt for Red October*. "He should like this."

"And what about you?" he asks. "What genre do you prefer?"

I finally face my interrogator who reminds me of a slightly aged Ethan Hawke. "I have a penchant for feminist fiction."

"Because you're a lesbian?" he asks. "Or because you need stories to assert your femaleness?"

As I stand open-mouthed, considering if I want to respond to his question, Jean sidles up next to me, waving a book. "Found more Emily poetry." She looks at my new friend and says, "Hi."

"Hi," he says with a cocked smile.

I wrap my arm in between Jean's arm. "I like stories which inspire me to have courage."

"Okay," he says. "So meet me for coffee in an hour. We'll compare the books we've picked out and have a discussion on courage."

"It's a date," Jean pipes in. "Just the three of us."

"A date," he says. "For New Year's afternoon."

After he walks away, Jean nudges me. "You big flirt. So much for being in love."

"I was NOT flirting with him," I say. "And if it wouldn't have been for you, I wouldn't have agreed to coffee in an hour. As far as I'm concerned, you can have your date with that man."

"Oh no," says Jean. "You're not backing out on me. He's cute. Like in an English major kind of way. I'll need you to queue me through the conversation." She holds up her book. "Suppose he was impressed with my book selection."

I shake my head as guilt creeps up. The man is attractive. Like this city. I shouldn't have coffee with him, but I'll do it for Jean's sake.

Looking back at the Tom Clancy novels, I pick up *Clear and Present Danger* and *Patriot Games*. All gifts for Nick.

Nick's Journal

APRIL 12, 1985

Went with Jim and Brad to Iowa State. Partied at Jim's brother's apartment all weekend. Sarah=not real happy. What the hell. Senior year. How often do I get to do stuff like this with my friends. I'll make it up to her.

I got up early this morning before anyone else was up. Tried to clean the mess, but it was pretty bad. So I left to check out the campus.

The town that was full of people last night was dead. I spotted a few students walking with book bags. I wondered if I'd be the same way, getting up early to study on Sunday mornings. I doubt it. But I did like walking around the campus. It felt kind of strange.

I met lots of people at the party. Some interesting. Some that thought they were interesting. Lots of pretty girls. Not all so interesting. I liked one named Jessica. The farm girl. Smart. Knows how to drive a tractor. And butcher chickens! I think she wanted something to happen. But I'm not a cheater. Still, I wonder if I didn't drop the ball.

The buildings on the campus impressed me. I went into the library. I kept thinking to myself, I wonder how many students appreciate going to college. There were mostly foreign student in library, studying. They *probably appreciate it.*

I walked around, acting like I was a student looking for a book. Opening books and placing them back as carefully as I could. Then I found the big mural. The Grant Wood project. I read about this in the admission stuff. It's really cool. There are these three panels with pioneers. One man is breaking up the soil with two draft horses. The background has a team of oxen—like they were replaced by the horses. On the other side of the painting is this woman giving the farmer a drink. I'm not much into art, but I totally got that painting. When I went to leave, there was this quote on the ledge of the staircase.

"When tillage begins, other arts follow. The farmers, therefore, are the founders of human civilization."

Pretty cool.

CHAPTER 40

NEW YEARS DAY

JANUARY 1993

Happy New Year's.

Oh sure, fireworks over Lake Michigan with a rocking band blasting is an okay way to celebrate, especially when your best friend invites a stranger from Borders who happens to be a University of Chicago cinematography professor to tag along. But I'm looking forward to a quiet night in the countryside with Nick. It's our own special New Year's celebration.

Nick boils the water for the spaghetti noodles as I stir the hamburger and Ragu for this extremely complex sauce. He's listening intently as I babble on about Chicago, avoiding the part about the professor in case there's any misinterpreting the situation as a flirtatious encounter. While the professor was somewhat charming, I played as standoffish as I could. For one, my mind kept tracking to Nick. And two, Jean was acting strangely smiley around this fellow, so I'm positive she likes him.

As we sit down to pile our plates with noodles, Nick says, "I've always wanted to visit Chicago. In the summer though, to catch a Cubs game."

"Cubs? I thought you were a Royals fan."

"I am, unfortunately. But there's this thing. Baseball people are...nostalgic. Wrigley field. Fenway. I hope to see those places someday."

After I slurp a large portion of my noodles, I mention, "Have I ever mentioned how much I love Chicago?"

Nick twirls spaghetti around with his fork. His eyebrows furrow, almost instantly. I feel terrible I brought it up. It's like I cheated on him. I'm ready to retract my words when he sniffs the air. Then I smell the pungent odor of burnt toast.

"The garlic bread!"

We jump to it, and Nick pulls the blackened bread from the oven. Cracking the window, Nick allows the the freezing temperatures to lunge after smoke.

"Gheesh," I say disappointedly. "I can't make a meal without screwing some part of it up."

"You know," he says picking up the bread. "I actually like burnt toast. It's the best way to eat it."

"You're just being nice."

"No, really. I'm being honest." He puts two pieces on his plate.

"Now, back to this idea of Chicago," he resumes the conversation. "Are you thinking of looking for a job there?"

Nick is a wall of stone–not appearing upset, sad, or happy about my possible endeavor.

"What do you think about it?"

Come on, Nick. Fight for me.

He shrugs. "It's your life."

"You're a big help." I pause while we continue to twirl and slurp noodles. "I'm unsure about lots of things. But I was always pretty certain about what kind of lifestyle I wanted after graduation. Now, I'm not sure at all."

"It's kind of like, ordering food at a restaurant."

I want to smile at him, but I can't. We're getting too close to my real future. He puts his fork down and turns to me.

"Amy? Do you remember when you promised me you wouldn't let me taint your decision when you looked for a job?"

"That would be entirely impossible."

"No, it would not. Whatever path you choose, do not consider me. If you start trying to put me in the formula, you'll end up processing loans the rest of your life."

"I don't mind processing loans," I say crossly. "Do you think I should move away?"

"If I could answer that question without influencing your career decision, I would."

We remain silent, except, of course, for the

slurping.

"Let's just enjoy the time we have together," he says quietly.

It sounds as if one of us is terminal. I don't say another word. Nick picks up a slice of burnt toast. As he takes a bite, the entire piece crumbles into tiny black granules in his hands.

"Yum. This is delicious."

I can't help but giggle. Soon we are both laughing hysterically. Then he grabs me, pulling me on to his lap. Once he begins to nibble on my ear, uttering, "Beyond adorable," talk of my future has safely crawled to the back of my mind.

CHAPTER 41
MONEY FOR NOTHING?

JANUARY 1993

Could this be fate? Or is my imagination working overtime? I have almost arrived to my first class of the semester, which happens to be Ethics, with something disturbing on my mind. Well, possibly disturbing. Maybe it's not disturbing at all.

But it's just not adding up.

Could my boss be a bad guy?

I think through the facts.

Regulators (the FDIC to be exact) have infiltrated our building.

They request lots of files.

They interview important staff members (not me).

I'm trying to make sense of an email I received from Roger (something I never get) requesting me to change the name on one of his loans to his mother's name. A commercial loan in the amount of $800,000 for cattle. Did I miss somewhere along the line that he had a cattle operation? And I can't mess with that type of loan without someone proofing my work. Doesn't he know that? But he asked me to keep confidential. Said he's particular about who knows his cattle venture. It feels all weird.

He's my boss. He hired me. Shouldn't I trust him to not lead me astray?

So why haven't I done anything yet?

Finally, after circling through these same questions over and over again, I arrive at the stark Eppley Building, which will host class tonight. As I walk toward the building, I remember thinking how fun my undergraduate Ethics class would be. Then we dove deep into the philosophies of those early Greek thinkers, probing the most profound questions of all humanity. An Aristotle (or was it Plato?) quote tugs at me right now. "Knowing yourself is the beginning of all wisdom." Maybe that's my psyche, telling me what to do about Roger's request.

CHAPTER 42

ANOTHER BRICK IN THE WALL

JANUARY 1993

When I arrive at work today, another email from Roger awaits me. He needs the maintenance done as quickly as possible–to run reports for the FDIC to show it's been done. So he says.

Per my intuition, I forward both of the emails to Ginny. Then I go to her office.

"Had a chance to read your email yet?" I ask her.

She articulates an enormous sigh. "Just pulling a bunch a crap for the FDIC. Roger wants me to hold off on running the commercial report for some reason."

Peeking over to Roger's office, I confirm his engagement with an examiner, so I shut the door. Ginnie's head flies up.

"What's going on?" she asks. A closed door means business around these parts.

I point to her computer. "Read your email.

Quickly."

As she reads, she groans in disbelief. Swiveling back to me, her eyes have awakened considerably. Then she gestures me over toward her computer.

"Did you research the history?" she asks. "Or is it restricted with an employee code?"

"No restrictions. For some reason. Although he told me very few employees knew of his cattle business."

Ginny navigates through the loan, making some notes on the dates and the collateral. "Oh no. Oh gosh. I have a feeling...Roger doesn't own cattle. You know what this is?"

"I looked, but I couldn't figure it out."

"Roger's strategy for making his loan growth goals every year. By putting fake loans on the books. Then paying them off after the first of the year when he gets his bonus."

"No way."

Ginny doesn't respond. "Last date of maintenance on this loan was right before Donna quit. She changed the loan back into his name. I bet she was doing all his maintenance work for him. Apparently, she had every intention of letting him get caught."

I straighten up, like a soldier ready to fight. "What do we do?"

Almost as soon as the words spill from my mouth, a tap comes at the door, and a head pops in. The head pops in. Roger stands in the doorway.

Behind him lurks a bank examiner–a lady wearing a smart red suit.

"Sorry to interrupt," he says. "Ginny, have you had a chance to run an updated commercial loan trial report?" He glances to me, with an unsteady eye.

Looking to the examiner, Ginny waves them both in. "Actually come in. We have a question."

Roger and the examiner take seats at the desk. Roger taps his foot.

"Amy and I were just looking at this commercial loan of yours, Roger. The one for your cattle? The one that needs maintenance?"

The examiner looks to Roger. "Is this why I'm still waiting for the employee loan list?"

Roger looks to be holding his breath. "It's not mine actually. It's my mother's. For cattle."

"Your mother runs a cattle operation? I'll definitely need to review that file, Roger. And why would the loan need maintenance? When did it get changed?"

Roger doesn't respond. He begins to scratch his head.

Ginny turns to her computer. "I can do a printout of the loan. And the email you sent to Amy about modifying the loan."

"Yes. I'll take all of that," says the examiner. "Roger, let's find that loan file and move to your office. I have more specific questions for you."

Roger's contorts, and melts to an ashen color

as he rises to follow the examiner. It's the first time I ever see him nervous and fidgety. And it's one of the last times I ever see him.

CHAPTER 43

BREAKDOWN

FEBRUARY 1993

Mom snaps into my room, showing me the news article labeled: FRAUDSTER. But I push it aside. I'm tired of it.

"I suppose that's why Donna quit, huh?" Mom asks. "She always did seem a little more stressed after Roger took over."

Mom continues to read while I attempt to study.

"Says here Jim Zee is the interim president. What's Ginny think of that?"

"She's fine with it," I lie. Ginny told me she felt passed over, but the board unanimously voted in Jim.

Mom puts the paper down. "Really? She's fine with it?" Mom shakes her head. "It doesn't surprise me she was passed over. The business world is a shark tank for women. Unless you have some real credentials. Like a law degree."

"Or an MBA."

"Right," Mom says more quietly. "I'll let you study."

I put away my finance book, which is obviously taxing my brain since it's throbbing. I pick up some lighter reading: marketing. Then I compare the textbooks. My hope? An inclination toward one of them will distinctly emerge as a career destination. While I kick ass in finance, I find marketing fascinating. Reading about companies and how they turn their products into a business is more like reading a juicy narrative for me. Executives get axed. New products are developed. Ad campaigns transform cultures. It's art. Not so much science.

Just as I dig into a company called "Schweppes," Nick calls.

"You sound tired," Nick says.

"My head's been busting me up almost all day."

"Stressed maybe?" Nick asks. "From all the shit that's been going down."

"Maybe I'm just exhausted," I say while trying to squeeze my head as the pain seems to increase precipitously with each word I attempt to say. "Need to finish... studying." My speech is beginning to trail off. "Call you tomorrow... "

After hanging up the phone, I lay on my bed, clutching my throbbing head. The pain won't let me sleep. My books and papers lay beside me, and I wonder if I should move them as I begin to feel nauseated.

Mom checks in on me after a bit. "You okay?"

I can't respond. The light blurs my vision. I stumble, forcing myself up to get to the bathroom as I feel vomit rise in the back of my throat. Mom catches my unsteadiness, leading me to the toilet. After throwing up, I only feel worse. My head pounds inside a constricting vice-grip.

Mom asks me questions which I can barely register, so I garble responses. Helping me back to my room, she guides me back down. Then she brings in a cold wash rag, which soothes for only a few seconds. I attempt to adjust myself into a comfortable position, but soon I'm limp. Tears stream down my cheeks. Something is exploding in my head.

Dad stomps in the room, too loudly, jarring every nerve in my body. "We're taking you to the ER."

An aneurism. A tumor. Something horrible is happening to me.

Someone mentions migraine. Family history. Words jumble. I don't care. About anything. I just want the pain to go away.

In a state of pain-induced fog, I find myself at the hospital, receiving shots that put me into a restless sleep, allowing me to lose track of time. I awake intermittently and eventually find myself feeling like a person again, only tired, sans the remarkable pain. Eventually, I wake up with the ability to communicate completely – something I had lost temporarily. I look to my parents and say, "Let's go home."

Amazingly, I have survived.

Offering gratitude to my parents takes all of my energy. I value my life. I've never had a suicidal thought. But now I understand how excruciating pain can make some people wish for death.

CHAPTER 44

BABYSITTING

MARCH 1993

"Why *did* you volunteer to do this?"

I'd like to think I would've made a good sister. Volunteering to babysit for the Catholic School's funding raising event of the season seems like a very sisterly act.

As soon as we walk in to Jim and Judy's, Josh zips through the living room in his Batman pajamas. Jim seems comfortably settled into the sofa.

"The kid's had bees in his butt all day," Jim mentions while his eyes don't dare sway from the television. Nick sits down and becomes instantly engaged in a basketball game. I am vaguely aware that March is an important time for college basketball.

"Hi, Josh!" I address the zippy boy.

He stops, puts his hands on his hips, and corrects me. "I'm Batman!"

Speeding for a few more laps around the

house, he dashes as closely to Nick as he can with a coy attempt to capture his attention. Nick snatches Batman to tickle him in a seemingly tortuous way. I'd intercede, but the three-year old is laughing, like a most charming hyena.

Judy emerges from the back bedroom with her hair bouncing in loose curls. While she always looks pretty, I'm not used to seeing her in a skirt and strappy heels. She's kind of a stunner, really.

Without much of a greeting she begins giving me strict babysitting instructions. I feel like I'm fifteen again.

"... and he needs to take D-Allergy before he goes to bed. It's already measured and sitting next to the sink here." She shows me the medicine and looks around, considering anything else she might have forgotten. "Feel free to eat whatever you can find. Josh ate a grilled cheese and applesauce about a half an hour ago, so he shouldn't be hungry for at least...another twenty minutes." She smiles.

"I think we can handle it." I reassure her.

"Oh! The phone number!" She finds the number and scribbles it down next to the phone. "Thanks so much. It's really great you guys are doing this. I'm not sure who's more excited! Me or Josh."

After some prying, Jim unglues his eyes from the TV and they leave.

I'm left now to observe the wrestling match which has now brought Nick to the floor while holding Josh in the air like a plane. The sweet image conjures thoughts of the future, and I can't help but think what a great daddy Nick will be.

"Ahhh! No Nickie, I'm gonna puke!" Josh says as he continues to giggle.

"You better not, you little monkey..."

And that's when it happens. Applesauce and chunks of cheese violently unleash over a sizable radius, centered on Nick's head. Nick bounds up, hands the vomiting Josh to me and sprints to the bathroom. I hold the convulsing boy in my lap as he continues to expel the now orange-tinted contents of his tummy on Judy's crème-colored carpet.

I try to comfort the boy, caressing his head. Josh looks at me with encrusted puke on his mouth, his big blue eyes watering, and confesses, "I tink I had a wet faht."

That would explain the warmth creeping through my jeans. I lift the boy up to confirm. Taking Josh to the bathroom where Nick has most recently vomited, we set up triage. Nick is now rinsing off his shirt in the sink.

"Josh!" Nick scolds. "Next time, tell me if you're gonna puke. That was freakin' gross."

"How can you blame him? You had to make tickling a sport."

I check to make sure Josh's feelings aren't hurt, but he looks to Nick and begins laughing. Once again, the hyena. It didn't even take tickling.

For the next hour, I give Josh a bath, wash poopy and vomit-stained clothing, and then scrub the carpet. Nick tries to help, but entertaining Josh, without tickling him, is his highest and best use. I'm wearing some of Judy's sweatpants, with a button-down flannel shirt, while my jeans are drying. It's almost as attractive as Nick in Jim's ill-fitting, barely-reaching-his-ankle sweatpants. "Nice knickers!" I say to him. Nick decides to go shirtless, so Josh insists on being shirtless as well.

After the commotion we sit on the couch to read. Well, I'm reading to Josh while Nick watches a different basketball game. Josh assails me with a plethora of questions; although I'm quite certain (certain as a jurtain) he has read these Dr. Suess books several times before.

Since his little head keeps bobbing, I ask Josh, "You tired?"

"No!" he says, rubbing his eyes.

"Didn't think so," I say. "But you can lay down on the couch if you want. Maybe we could pop in a video."

"Say what?" says Nick, glaring daggers into me.

"Yeah!" agrees Josh. "*Rescuers Down Under!*"

"It's only basketball," I say to Nick.

He throws up his hands.

We begin the movie, and Josh is sleeping within fifteen minutes.

"We can watch the game now, Nick."

Nick smiles at the animated albatross. Then he shrugs. "You can finish this if you want."

I was actually nodding off myself, but will allow Nick to think it's my fault he's missing basketball.

We finish watching the movie, as I try hard to swallow my tears. Come on, Amy! Who cries at *Rescuers Down Under*? I peek to see if Nick has any tears.

He stretches his arms. "Whoa. I was nodding off there at the end!"

"You didn't cry?"

He laughs. "Cry? Over that?" Then he inspects me. "Don't tell me you did!"

Jim and Judy return soon after the movie with questioning looks. I hope they don't notice my tears. "What's up with the sweats?" Judy asks.

After recounting our evening, Judy says, "Sounds like you had more fun than we did."

"The simple joys of raising a child!" Jim says, while patting Nick on the back.

Joy? Sure. Simple? Not so much.

CHAPTER 45

WONDERFUL TONIGHT

APRIL 1993

"You look really nice," I say, navigating myself, in my short dress, into Nick's pickup. "But did I mention the wedding is at the bar?"

"You think I'm overdressed?" Nick pulls at his tie. "Glad I spent the last hour working on this noose."

"Carissa will appreciate the effort."

Nick takes off his tie and tosses it on the dashboard. "You're wearing a dress. You're kinda fancy too."

"Floral dress. It's casual."

"Pardon me." Nick shakes his head while pulling away. "All these rules. I asked the twins what to wear, and they said–"

Twins!

"You didn't tell them Carissa was getting married at The Foxy, did you?"

Nick sinks his head into his shoulders. "Yeah. Maybe not my best idea."

"Do you think they'll show up?

"I have no doubt," Nick says. "I wouldn't worry too much about it. The Foxy's always busy on a Saturday night. They'll get lost in the crowd."

I wonder though.

"Just so you know, this will be my first bar wedding. Not everyone in my family makes a habit of this practice. Actually, I'm excited for you to meet more of my family. Especially Bruce. He's a city boy. Grew up in Des Moines."

"Does he talk farming?"

"He's very agreeable to talking just about anything," I say.

We arrive at the bar, occupied with patrons seemingly comfortable sitting in their positions. Wedding invitees are easy to spot, as they notched up their natty. Nick gets caught up with a few fellows as I attempt to drag him across to the apparent threshold of where the wedding celebration begins. Finally we find ourselves at the corner of the bar, where my first relative of the evening appears to be waiting for us.

"Bruce! You. Look. Amazing."

I hug my cousin as he teeters with some sort of tawny cocktail on the rocks. He kisses me on the cheek like a best girlfriend.

"Oh kitten," he says. "You never change, do you? And I'm stating that as a compliment, dear. Really." He gives Nick a flagrant up-and down inspection. "So, tell me about this."

"*This* is my friend, Nick Klein."

Nick extends his hand to Bruce who dons a silky purple shirt with deep navy trousers. His sleek hair is coiffed like a GQ model, and he has bathed himself in an abundance of something appetizing like Calvin Klein's *Obsession for Men*.

"Aren't you a cutie-patootie?" Bruce pushes Nick's hands away in favor of a warm hug and peck on the cheek.

Nick stiffens, and replies in a deeper-than-usual voice, "Nice to meet you."

"And it's fabulous to meet you!" Bruce turns to me. "Wait until you see Carissa. She's stunning. I helped her find the dress." He takes a drink and chinks his ice. "And while I hate to brag, too much, I also designed her jewelry."

"I'm sure she'll be the belle of the ball," I say. "Or maybe like the belle of the bar."

We chat about Bruce's job as a shoe salesmen in Des Moines and his dream of becoming an artist. That's when I notice Penny, Deb, and Connie enter the bar. Penny has a dour expression. Tapping Nick, I interrupt the conversation to excuse myself.

"Carry on. I need to say a quick hello to my bank friends." Nick gives me a "please don't leave me" look, so I provide a reassuring rub on his shoulder before I leave him with my cousin.

"Hey!" I say to my bank friends who are searching for a table. "Girls night out?"

Pink rims Penny's eyes. Her posture is slumped. She's wearing her black-framed glasses.

"I left Jeff," she say. "Big blowout. I had it this time."

Deb chomps on her gum. Connie gives me the slightest of nods as if to say, "Yep. She really left the douche bag."

I give Penny a hug. "You okay?"

"I don't know," she says. "It's probably a dumb idea to go out. Is there a party going on here?"

I release myself, shaking my head. "No, not really."

Penny looks me up and down. "Why are you so dressed up?"

"Oh. Well, my cousin's getting married."

"Here?" Deb asks.

I don't respond, but watch Penny's reaction – hoping the idea of a wedding won't upset her.

She drops her head, hiding her hands in her face. Connie begins to rub her back, just as Penny slaps her hands to her knees and bursts out into blood hoisting laughter.

The dam has bursted. We're all laughing. I'm not even all that amused by my cousin getting married in the bar, but I don't want to dampen Penny's spirit any more.

"Join the wedding guests for a drink." I point

to Bruce and Nick. The disparity in the two men is apparent. "I think my guy would like a little company."

As we join Nick and Bruce, Bruce holds his glass up to the girls and asks, "Did the party just begin?"

We share introductions and drinks, then erase any awkwardness with Karaoke stories, which probably aren't terribly interesting. But the booze makes everything sort of fascinating. As I glance to where we typically perform, I spot my parents sitting in a corner with Grandma Ruby–next to the make-shift stage which has been narrowly transformed with some pink tulle. Since Bruce has acclimated to the girls, I try to pull Nick away to say hello to Grandma. But he tells me he'll be right over. Bruce owes him a tequila shot.

"Grandma!" I say pulling up a red vinyl seat next to her. "I've never seen you in a dress."

"This is what you bury me in." The sleeveless denim embroidered jumper shows off her small snake tattoo coiled on her forearm. "I don't get any fancier than this."

"What if you die in the winter?" Dad asks.

Grandma turns to me. "Your boyfriend there is almost too good-looking."

"Thank you!"

"I don't mean that as a compliment, sweetie." She takes hold of my arm. "Your grandfather was too good-looking and I swear to God I followed that man around like a puppy dog. And look where it got me. Living in a trailer in the woods."

"Grandma!" I say turning to her. "I thought you loved it there."

"I do. Now. But you got yourself some pretty big dreams there with that MBA thingy. And that boy over there is awfully handsome."

I glance over to see him toasting with Bruce and the rest of the girls. He is *awfully handsome.* Then he slams his shot glass down and makes his way over, sitting down next to me–now feeling all googly-eyed because of my Grandma's sweet sentiments.

"I like your family," he says to the table.

"Nice to see you too, Nickie," says Grandma Ruby.

As Grandma and Nick banter, I watch Penny drinking with Bruce and the bank tellers. She still looks sad. I need to do something for her. An idea strikes.

"I think we should set Penny up with Chris," I say.

"Chris? As in Fekes?" he asks.

As he gives me a gives me a questioning look, my Aunt Kathy rushes out of the back room to announce we're about to begin. Bruce ushers the banking girls over to his table of family members. They wave to me and smile.

Once Kathy sits down, the stage is taken over by a droopy Justice of the Peace and a smiling guy in a suit.

"I know him," I say. "How do I know him?"

"You didn't tell me she was marrying Chad Hicks," says Nick.

From the Care Center. I hadn't put it together after seeing the invitation.

"She's marrying that nurse! Good for her."

Kathy signals to her husband, my Uncle Bob. Once he pushes the jukebox buttons, Bryan Adams croons the words *Everything I Do, I Do it For You.*

Out of the back room steps a little girl–who wears a bright pink ribbon around a small pinch of hair. Her silk dress sweeps the floor as she trots straight to the groom with a scowl on her face.

Then comes Carissa who looks like she has come straight from a Victoria Secret's shoot in her low-cut, gold lamé evening gown. The haltered dress accentuates her smooth, dark complexion (defying her Scandinavian roots). Undoubtedly, she's selling that rose tattoo on her left shoulder. Her black hair is loosely pulled up with strands sweeping across her pretty face. Despite her sketchy past, at this moment, I can't help but feel proud, and hopeful, for my cousin. There is a hush, and a few "wowies" across the bar as everyone admires her. Even Nick doesn't hold back a "Whoa."

The ceremony begins as we hear more people trample into the bar. Everyone, including the bride and groom, can't help but glance at the door every time it opens. But my breath actually hiccups when

I notice Jake and Will making their entrance. They beam obnoxious smiles. They wave big. For a moment, I see Will purposefully spread his hands out directly to Carissa, who giggles and returns back to her place in the ceremony.

Nick lowers his head and whispers, "They are *not* my cousins." I find this comment ironic.

Jake and Will clamor to a place at the bar which isn't terribly far from our table. I hear Jake ask, "Is that Chad Hicks? She's marrying him? I thought he died of an overdose!"

Nick buries his chin into his neck.

Finally, once the bride and groom are presented, thunderous cheers and applause erupt–all throughout the bar.

That's when shots infinitude and dancing delirious begin. Nick dances like I've never seen before. He dances with my mother, my grandmother, Penny, and even Bruce.

Nick and I take a break from the dance floor to introduce Jake to Penny, since they seem to be edging toward each other at the bar. They easily strike up a conversation which centers around unique dance moves. On the other side of the bar I catch Will flirting with Carissa while Chad is having a discussion with my grandma. I point this out to Nick.

"Not good," he says. "We better take action."

Breaking into the conversation, I force myself between the bride and Nick's cousin. Will glowers at me, which dissolves soon enough when Chad pokes his head in and says,"Hey, baby!" Pulling her close, Carissa gives him the same smile she's been giving Will.

The bride and groom skip off to dance and Will orders two shots as I say, "Only two? There are three of us standing here."

"These are for me. To drown my sorrow. My lost love."

"You poor guy," I begin to say as a commotion ensues behind us.

"What the–" Will says, rushing up to the other side of the bar. Nick follows right behind.

On the other side of the bar, Jeff (Penny's Jeff!) is holding Jake against the wall screaming in his face, "You been fucking around with her?"

Jake stares straight through Jeff, then gives Will a quick sideward glance. "No, man. I really don't want any trouble."

"You lying to me, shithead?"

"Why would I lie to you, dude?"

Jeff pounds the wall next to Jake's head. "To avoid getting the shit kicked out of you!"

"I'm not worried about you kicking the shit out of me," says Jake. "If I was worried about that, I wouldn't be trying to screw your girlfriend. Who, by the way, kind of likes me."

Will drops his head, uttering "Dumb ass" just as Jeff lands his punch. But Jake ducks just enough, so that he barely receives a hit. Jake launches his body against Jeff, tackling him to the ground.

Penny screams. Will turns to Nick. "You gotta help me stop this. Or the military will shit can him."

Will jumps in, pulling Jake off. Once Jeff is free, he hops up to attack Jake again, but Nick pulls him back. Jeff turns around and slugs Nick in the nose. Blood squirts everywhere.

I scream just as Nubbie, the bar owner, steps in, holding a taser and shouts, "Stop you mother fuckers! The police are on their way right now."

Everyone in the bar turns into statues, except for Nick's who's holding his face, oozing of blood.

"Can I get him a rag?" I ask.

Nubbie throws Nick a towel from the bar. Then holding the taser, he walks up to Jeff. "How many times have I had to kick you outta here?"

Jeff stares him down. "You didn't call the cops. You never do. You know they'll get you for something else."

"I've been waiting to use this taser."

Jeff is breathing heavy, then says to Nick. "My fight wasn't with you Klein." Then he looks to Jake. "You. Stay out of my business."

Jeff walks over to Penny. Grabbing her by the arm he says, "Let's go."

Wiggling away from him, Penny stomps over between Jake and Will. "You go."

Jeff throws his hands in the air. "You wanna be a whore? Be a whore. I ain't ever taking you back. Stupid bitch."

"I don't feel a need to respond to you anymore," says Penny, clutching on to Jake's arm.

"Fine," says Jeff. "Hope those cupie twins can support you and your dumb bank job then. Don't come crying to me when you need money."

Jeff stomps out, shoving people out of his way as he leaves. I turn to check on Nick's injured status. As he removes his bloodstained towel, I try to assess if his nose has been deformed, without throwing up. Black and blue circles have formed under both of his eyes and a lump has grown on his nose. A crowd forms around us while my Aunt Kathy, who's a nurse, bustles her way right next to me.

"Yep," she says. "It's broken. Does it hurt?"

"Stings a little," says Nick. "Luckily, I've had plenty of tequila tonight."

"Well, it's not going anywhere," says Aunt Kathy. She turns to the crowd. "Let's watch the bride and groom cut their cake before anything else happens."

Nick smiles at me, shrugging. Nubbie gives him a bag of ice and we congregate to watch Carissa and Chad slice into a cake using a butcher knife. Penny sneaks up behind us and says, "Hey. Thanks for taking a punch for me tonight." Then she gives him a hug. "No one has ever done that for me."

Jake takes Penny's hand. "I would've. But I'm much quicker than Nick."

She smiles at Jake, then pats his cheek.

"Where's Will?" I ask.

Jake shakes his head. "Couldn't stand watching Carissa and Chad any longer. Feel defeated."

"At least he didn't get his nose broken tonight," says Nick.

Nick becomes the hero of the night. After the cake-cutting, everyone insists on buying him a drink for his courage under fire. Even Grandma Ruby buys him a shot and makes him dance with her again. By the end of the night, he is utterly wasted.

I am ready to drive him home, since I switched to tea hours ago. That's when the first few notes of Eric Clapton's *Wonderful Tonight* begin. Even though he can barely stand or speak, he is desperate to dance. When he takes me into his arms, I feel his strength, his goodness, and his extreme drunkenness. He's still endearing to me.

I drop into his chest. The moments of the night swirl in my head. I consider what happened to Penny and Jeff and wonder if they ever felt this way about each other. Would we ever grow resentful of each other? I can't imagine.

"My darling, you look wonderful tonight..."

Nick sings to me. His singing is awful. His voice wavers between octaves. He has no pitch. He barely remembers the words, and when he does, he slurs.

I'm dancing with a broken-nosed man, in his drunken stupor, at a wedding in a bar. But I wouldn't want to be anywhere else at this moment. Then he stops his singing and grabs my shoulders. Spilling out words to me I will never forget, he says,

"You must be what true love feels like, Amy. I've never been happier."

He didn't even slur.

CHAPTER 46
PENNY LANE

APRIL 1993

"How's Nick?"

I explain to Penny how his nose isn't broken–not even fractured. His punch from Jeff got him a nice lump, but no broken bones. Along with all his sympathy shots on Saturday night, he was a hurting mess the next day, enduring "possibly the worst hangover he ever remembered." His sorry state caused a noticeable absence in church, and a stern phone call from Helen.

Penny apologizes, sort of.

"Don't you worry about Nick," I say. "He's a tough kid."

She turns to her computer, as if she's going to end the conversation. But I'm not ready to let her off the hook.

"So, you seem to be interested in a wonder

twin?"

Her face flies up. "I'm not rushing into anything right now." She taps on her computer. "But he
is cute."

"What's your plan, Pen?" I ask. "Now that
you're not with Jeff. You sticking around Fox
Plaine?"

"I have no plans of quitting a secure job with
insurance," she says. "That's for sure."

I reposition myself to face her directly. "Maybe
you should consider taking some classes now. Get
your degree."

She looks up at me and blinks. "I have my
degree."

"Oh," I swallow. *Do I know this?*

She lets out a long breath and begins to type.

"What's your degree in again?"

"Don't you have work to do?" she asks.

Nodding agreeably, I turn away. But within a
few steps from her desk, she says, "It was just a foot
in the door. This job."

I turn back. "What do you really want to do
then?"

"Something like Ginny. Manage people. Maybe
do some loans. But I suppose only so many of us can
do certain positions."

"Have you ever told anyone?" I ask.

"I told Roger. Five million times. He always
said I'd just have to watch out for the right opportunity. But with Ginny being so young, he was never

sure when or what that would be."

"There were no other career options for you?"

"A few other jobs have come around," she says looking up at me. "But he always liked me in this role."

I glance at the corner office. "Get over there and talk to our new leader. Tell him you want to do something more."

She sits back, taking off her glasses. Pink frames. "I've had a pretty eventful week. Not sure if I have it in me right now."

"You can do it!" I demand. "You know what I did this morning before work? I studied for a test and cleaned dog shit off my bedroom carpet. We women can do anything."

Penny places her glasses back on, folds her arms together, and stares ahead for a moment. When the phone buzzes, she hollers at Deb to take it.

"Cleaned dog shit, huh? Well..." She looks back into the corner office. "Maybe you're right. I know I could've, should've been given a chance at some of those jobs."

"Go and talk to Jim," I say as I begin my trek back to my desk. Then she stops me one more time.

"By the way, Jake invited me to do some target shooting with him."

"Seems like a strange activity for a first date."

"Strange guy. Twice he's called to sing Penny Lane to me today," she says. Then her lips swell into a smile. "But I don't mind."

CHAPTER 47

HOLD ON FOR ONE MORE DAY

JULY 1993

The theme for tonight: female empowerment.

"All songs sung must somehow reflect our inner Gloria Steinem," I announce.

So Deb and Linda march to the Foxy stage, ready to wail *Walk Like an Egyptian*. I don't get how this song empowers, but The Mothers seem to be oozing boldness over the idea.

Once their eyes focus on the monitor, I turn to Penny.

"You upset? About not getting the loan officer gig?"

"Sort of," she says without so much of a shrug. "But," she faces me, " I requested permission to attend lending school. Since that was the reason they didn't pick me."

"And?"

"After a little fussin, because of the cost, Jim said ok."

"Nice!" I say, patting her on the shoulder.

"Why didn't you apply, Amy? I thought when Jim told me I didn't get it, he was going to say it was given to you."

I couldn't apply knowing you were applying.

"Need to focus on getting my MBA right now." I take a long drink. "Anyway, I've been interviewing with other companies."

"With who? Around here?"

I shake my head. *None around here.*

"I interviewed with the Federal Reserve Bank. In Kansas City. Next week I have two more interviews. A marketing company out of Chicago. And Commercial Federal Bank in Omaha."

"I think you should just stay working for us. Aren't you in love with Nick anyway?"

I am that. I am in love. But that love has insisted I not let him impact my career path.

CHAPTER 48

GET A REAL JOB

JULY 1993

"The Fed rejected you, huh?" Dad asks as we dine on a tasty lunch of olive loaf sandwiches together.

"I totally messed up the final interview," I explain. "Didn't know our legislators. Started making up names."

"Seriously? You don't know?"

"I know *now*," I say flipping through the newspaper. "Lesson learned. Test me on something. Like Clinton's staff members. Just to make sure I'm well-informed."

"Maybe you could put down a few of your novels."

I point to the newspaper. "See this?"

"Horoscope?"

"And other things."

He bites into his sandwich. "What about the

other companies? Anything else sound promising?"

"Just waiting to hear back."

"Got a preference?"

"Whichever one offers me a job."

A three star day, again. I fold up the news-paper without reading the text of my horoscope.

"If I go to work for Hinkley, I'll be working in marketing. In Chicago–doing creative, awesome stuff. Maybe even writing some jingles. Jean and I could even live together again."

"What about the bank in Omaha?"

"Treasury Analyst."

"Sounds important."

"It does. Kind of. A $6 billion bank has a few more layers than a $100 million dollar community bank."

"And the pay?"

"Not sure, but I've read that MBA grads start in the mid $40,000 range."

"Oh sure. Did you read that in your horo-scope?"

"I'm already working for pennies."

Getting up to clear my plate, my dad asks me to pass him the stack of mail, which I've already sifted through. As he thumbs through the letters, he pauses at one particular envelope.

"Did I miss something?"

"Commercial Federal," he says abruptly while handing me the letter. Someone has just kicked me in the stomach. "Sorry, Amy."

I open the letter and read through the standard reject language, searching for any snippet of positivity in the verbiage. But there is nothing but formatted text.

"But my interviews went so well."

"It's a tough job market."

"They did say they had over four-hundred applicants, but I felt I really connected with the interviewer."

Am I that bad at reading people?

"There's still the marketing company."

I head back to work with a knot in my stomach. Chicago. It's a long way from here. It's a long way from Nick.

CHAPTER 49
IN BLOOM

JULY 1993

Mom would be amused to see my hands all soiled from this gardening adventure. Especially since I usually have ingenious excuses to avoid weeding her gardens. Like napping. Needless to say, here I am. Taking a break from thinking about finals and jobs. And how could I deny an invitation from Helen?

My knees twist in the dirt as I weed and pick vegetables with my boyfriend's mom. The smell of the fresh soil hits me like I just jumped in a puddle. I take off my gloves, wet from the morning dew to sift the dirt through my fingers.

"They didn't name our county after the soil for no reason, did they?" Helen asks.

"Huh?"

"Loam. Rich soil."

"Oh yeah," I say, pretending to be all up in our county's agricultural history.

Helen has become a professor, educating me on gardening. While my mother has attempted to get me interested in this hobby before, I'm actually listening today. Probably because Helen's not my mother. And Helen's is crazy passionate about vegetation. Take these tomato plants. The fruits are super-sized monster beef-steaks! Apparently, Helen doesn't just go to any old nursery to buy some start-up plant. She starts seeds in egg craters in February. That's what real gardeners do. She said so.

Dark wooden railroad ties, arranged with tall orange marigolds mark the entrance of her happy garden. Beyond her gated tomato plants, the plushy plot is marked with radishes, carrots, onions, potatoes, cucumbers, and rows of tall sweet corn. I spot two raised, leafy beds to the right of the rowed garden. Helen stomps to one of the beds, pulling up a strawberry, gesturing for me to come.

"Watch out for the sneaky garters," she says. "They like to hide in here."

I stop. "I'm fine right here."

She laughs. "You don't wanna see my pumpkins?" She asks pointing to the other bed with the large, leafy vines.

I tiptoe to the pumpkin patch, leery of what serpentine creature I might find. Once I'm there, however, I become swept up in the smell of Halloween as I see the tiny flowers that will become gourds hiding the leaves.

I search my vast perimeter. Beyond the garden is an entire orchard of trees, with fluttering leaves and chirpy birds. I'm guessing the trees bear apples and other fruits. Maybe apricots. Cherries. Helen has created her own slice of Eden.

"It's like a whole other farm here," I say. "Beautiful."

"Don't I know it."

I ask Helen if she plans to take any of her food to the Farmers Market.

"Hell no," Helen says. "We can most of it."

Canning. My mother has never taught me the art of this Iowa tradition. Should I play stupid?

"My girls hate me for it," Helen continues. "I imagine you hate canning as well."

I just smile.

"Enough of this," Helen commands. "Time to visit the flowers."

Helen initiates the tour wearing her straw hat, cropped pants, patterned cotton shirt, and pink apron which hosts a cache of gardening tools. Beyond the neatly trimmed bushes, she has planted a variety of roses and lilies throughout her yard. Helen teaches me stuff. Yellow Trumpets. Orange Tigers. Pink Stargazers. White Stargazers. There's even a large red hibiscus plant growing on her front porch, and I'm amused at the tropical essence on this very rural farm. Large clay and stone pots set on the patio, mixed with cascading flowers or saluting foliage. I learn of varigated geraniums and double wave petunias and decide that pale yellow can be just as brilliant as bright purple. Suddenly, I'm bitten. I want to be a gardener.

"Here," Helen pulls out some shears, and leads me to an area she considers her wildflowers near the back. "We're gonna cut some of these daisies and phlox. Before they kill my yard." She continues to snip. I cringe, thinking about the gap she's leaving. But as she cuts, I notice the beds look unscathed. "These'll look nice on your mom's table, don't ya think?"

She hands me a bunch. "Could take some for Dave," she says. "The nurses will appreciate the gesture."

After collecting an armload of the friendly white and fragrant violet flowers, Helen stretches back up and asks, "You hungry?"

"Starved!" I say, but inspired.

Helen and I sneak inside to eat ham sandwiches, macaroni salad, brownies, and lemonade. I'm on my second ham sandwich as she nibbles on her first.

"I can't believe how hungry I am!" My stomach has been growling, practically chewing me out for the past hour.

"Manual labor works up an appetite, don't it?"

The incorrect grammar is like nails on a chalkboard to me, but I have been learning to forgive. It's quite prevalent in Loam County. I just nod and say,

"Sure does," wondering if I should say, "sure do" so not to sound haughty.

As we sit at the kitchen table, I look at a Grant Wood painting in the living room.

"I like your painting."

"Grant Wood?" Helen pulls herself up to consider the image of two women planting midst a vast and simple countryside. "*Springtime in the Country.* That's what it's called. Nick gave it to me for my birthday a few years ago. Every once in awhile, my son surprises me."

I smile to myself, thinking how Nick agonizes over gift-giving. But the painting seems profoundly thoughtful. The neat and congruent lines remind me of the Klein's. Clean. Neat. Unpretentious.

"People are too busy these days," she says. "The picture reminds me how good it feels to take the time to get your hands dirty."

"Mom always tells me how gardening is therapeutic." I don't tell Helen how in college I'd toss our house plants in the garbage if I got tired of watering them.

"As you grow older, you seek out this kind of therapy." Helen smiles at me. "Someday you'll see."

I think I already do.

Once I arrive home from Helen's, I'm not feeling quite so terrible about having only one good job prospect.

A crazy idea even occurs to me.

What if Nick proposes to me and I become a full-time farm wife, like Helen, tending to gardens and learning to make meals?

I look to my Applied Management book sitting on the bed.

Bad idea. Silly, stupid, crazy idea. Too much sun.

I laugh out loud.

The phone rings.

The Human Resources representative from Commercial Federal is on the line.

"Amy, we'd like to make you an offer as a treasury analyst–"

I'm confused. Didn't I receive a rejection letter? I interrupt Ms. Human Resources.

"Uh, are you sure? I mean, I'm flattered, but it's just that I received a rejection letter last week.

"Oh, no! Not another one," she says. "We discovered a few rejections went out that shouldn't have. We thought we notified everyone. I'm so sorry..."

A job offer! Close to home. Placing my three pigs next to my night stand was ingenious. I hang up and dance and sing *Joy to the World* despite the season. I have a bona fide job offer. From a six billion dollar bank. What was I saying a few minutes ago? About becoming a full-time farmers wife? Crazy talk.

CHAPTER 50

ANTICIPATION

AUGUST 1993

I'm sitting here in bed, thinking.

I graduated from Creighton on Saturday. I now have my MBA. The pomp and circumstance was actually pretty nice. I had no idea Warren Buffett was going to speak. Mom almost seems proud of me. Heck, it's not every day she suggests we go to The Olive Garden to celebrate.

Nick was unusually quiet. Of course, he was congratulatory, but I sensed his distance. I can't decide if he's mad about the possibility of me going away, or just preparing for me to go away.

Then today I get the phone call.

"Come work for us in Chicago," says Wes Hinkley. "Marketing seems like a natural fit for you. We need a musician. And if I remember right, you're an

MBA graduate now?"

Starting pay: $32,000 with a raise review in six months. Hiring bonus: $4,000. Commercial Federal offered me $35,000. No hiring bonus, but annual bonuses based on performance.

I have a decision to make.

CHAPTER 51
THE ROAD

AUGUST 1993

Sitting in an Omaha coffee shop, full of professionals in their spiffy suits and dresses, I'm making a list of pros and cons of each job offer. One of my lucky pigs sits directly in front of me. The list of pros and cons should provide me clarity. Do pros and cons ever provide clarity? Right now, it's all I got.

Dreamy creative job. Dream city.

Or,

Lucrative, fancy, finance job. City near love of my life. (I'm not supposed to consider that factor, but it can not be helped.)

At one time in my life (like last year), this decision would've been a no-brainer. Part of me feels upset with myself.

Leaving Java Joe's after wasting forty-five minutes of arguing with myself, I catch a reflection in the window and notice how ratty my hair looks.

The salon next door seems to be calling my name.

The girl at the appointment desk reviews the schedule, studies the room of stylists and customers, then looks at me with a perky head tilt. "Actually, I can take you now."

My stylist's straight jet-black hair, makes me wonder if I could pull something like that off. When she asks me what I want, I feel embarrassed to say "Make me look like you!", so instead, I reply, "Oust me of this frizzy hairdo. Something more polished."

"I got this," she says with a smile. "Do you trust me?"

I nod easily, trusting her because she's pretty. But after she begins snipping away large chunks, I find myself holding my breath.

"You look nervous," she says.

"I'm fine," I lie.

She continues to snip away and I've resorted to sitting on my hands to control my anxiety. At least this hair bit has made me push my job dilemma to the back of my mind. Now, I'm more concerned about becoming bald.

"Almost done," she says while spritzing something on my hair before spinning me around before the mirror.

Ah!

I'm pleasantly surprised! My hair now bounces with some undiscovered shimmer in its new bobbed state.

The stylist frames my face. "Small face. Big

eyes. Perfect for this cut."

I leave the salon, feeling a small weight lifted from me, despite the impending decision.

I meander through a few other stores. A used book store. A vintage clothing store. A record store, where I stay too long eavesdropping on the shop worker's knowledge of up and coming music. I only leave when he tries to seduce me into a conversation about Pearl Jam.

On the way to my car, I pause at the window of a photographer's gallery. Simon Lee's Gallery. A large black and white print of a windmill catches my attention. I step inside.

Glancing around the store, I notice an area devoted to Omaha.

I linger over a musician playing the sax on a street corner. His eyes are closed, as if he's unaware of his surroundings which have been blurred in the shot. The next photo I notice is of a mass of children on a soccer field with parents filling the sidelines. Who, except parents, would ever purchase this piece, I wonder. The kids are cute, I guess. Then, I turn to a huge, panoramic picture showing off the downtown Omaha skyline. Only one skyscraper juts out among a color-imploded sunset. This would look nice in a bank.

Simon Lee has many collage photos. Fruit. Feet. A junkyard. Kids playing in the park. An unmade bed. I find a picture labeled "8:00 AM on Michigan Avenue." A crowd of people hustle through the sidewalk. One woman is kneeling to check something on the ground. A man is holding coffee in one hand and presumably his daughter in the other. They're the only two smiling in the crowd. I'm tempted to make the purchase and send to Jean. But it cost $129. Too pricy.

On my way out the door, I find a small photo almost hidden in the corner of the store. A cow licks her newly-born calf. Only the tongue and part of the mother's face can be seen as the new calf stares directly into the camera. It reminds me of the day Nick and I pulled that calf together.

Maybe it's sign. I almost didn't see it.

CHAPTER 52

FADE TO BLACK

AUGUST 1993

On my way home, I sing with Bono. *I will follow.*

Bono? What would you do?

Would Nick follow me to Chicago?

I know he wouldn't. How could he? He's established. He loves farming. I feel it every time he heads out to the field or anytime he tells me he has a new calf. Yet, farming is kind of a bi-polar kind of life. There are times he's not himself. He becomes a wall. And it's dangerous business! Who knows what could happen to him? And he's never explored anything else. Maybe he wants to, deep down. Maybe that's why he's not interfering with the decision.

What should I do? Hinkley. Commercial Federal.

Marketing. Banking.

Omaha. Chicago. Omaha. Chicago. Omaha.

Chicago.

Nick. Nick?

My head begins to throb the more I think about it.

I turn off the music.

The throbbing intensifies. A pain sears behind my left eye. I grab my head in attempt to mitigate the throbbing.

My exit is near. I need to get home. My vision begins to blur. I can do nothing but clutch my head as my elbow slides against the window.

Then, without warning, a shadow leaps before me.

A deer!

My reflexes rebound, and I quickly swerve to the left, not knowing if anyone is in the other lane. Now I'm headed directly toward another deer! I slam on the brakes.

SCREECHING. THUMP. GLASS SHATTERS.

All goes black.

Nick's Journal

August 1993

I had a strange dream.

A faceless person wearing a graduation gown was walking around in the Iowa State library. He stood in front of a large mural that looked like our machine shed. Then the mural turned into a real machine shed. The person turned into me and I was holding Dad's hand. Dad was all young. But I wasn't. He pointed inside and said, "Be careful. Your mother would never forgive me if anything happened to you." I looked inside and it was my old dirt bike.

That actually happened. My dad got me a dirt bike even though he made me think he would never buy me one. It was a great day. I understood then that my father was not afraid to let me live a life even though something terrible had happened to Dave.

Now, here I sit, in the middle of the night, in my bed looking out the window while the moon is nearly full, thinking about Amy.

I'm not afraid to love her anymore. I can hardly help it. But I'm not sure what the right thing to do is.

CHAPTER 53
ALIVE AND KICKING

AUGUST 1993

I'm awakened by voices hemming in on me.

"Why was she in Omaha?"

My father.

"She told me she wanted to do some shopping."

My mother.

"To celebrate? Did she take either of those jobs?"

"No. I believe she just wanted to think. Not sure why she wanted to go shopping." A pause. "Except she likes to shop."

"What happened to her hair?"

"Don't know. Maybe they had to cut it in the ER."

Slowly I lift my eyelids, and the ten pounds that weigh on them.

"She's awake," Dad points out to Mom who comes tripping to my side. Nick lingers in the back of the room.

"How do you feel sweetie?" Mom caresses my face.

"Groggy," I say. "I think I hit a deer."

"We know."

"Did the deer die?" I ask.

"Most likely."

"I tried to miss it." The news of the deer dying makes my stomach plunge.

"Your car's not so great either," adds Dad. "Gonna take a lot of duct tape to make the Buick presentable."

"Who cares about the car," Mom says. "Amy's okay."

I touch the stitches on my forehead. I try to raise my right arm. It's fully bandaged.

"No internal bleeding," continues my mother. "No broken ribs or anything like that."

"It feels like my face is deformed."

"Looks like it too," says Dad with a smile.

As I start to giggle, pain shoots through my body. I glance at Nick who seems to be working on a forced smile.

"Just a tad swollen," Mom says while rubbing my shoulder. "Ten stitches on the top of your forehead. But oh my. Your right arm. Thirty-one internal stitches and thirty-six external stitches. The police thought maybe the deer's hoof hit the window and shattered it. You probably put your arm up to protect yourself, like this." Mom demonstrates. Then she pivots in to stare at me, allowing her eyes to fill with tears. "I'm just so glad you're here."

Dad pats the top of my bandages. "Me too, Amos."

Nick has edged closer, now biting his lip.

"Did I get you out of the field?" I ask.

"I'm not in the field yet," he says shaking head with a half-smile, as if he's told me this before. "Getting equipment ready. But it doesn't matter. I actually stopped at the house to grab a sandwich when your mom had the message on the machine about your accident. Maybe the machine wasn't such a bad idea after all. Some messages are worth getting."

"So, can I go home now?" I ask.

"The doctor wants you stay overnight for observation. Mostly for your concussion."

Mom and Dad begin to chat about how long they should stay as I feel my eyelids drift. Nick grabs my hand, and I squeeze it for awhile. As I listen to my mother's voice, I feel the lilt of her inflections luring me back to sleep.

CHAPTER 54

IF YOU LEAVE

AUGUST 1993

I jolt up, disoriented.

The hospital room is dark, except for a light shining from a small lamp on the other side of my bed. The nurse is taking my blood pressure.

"You okay, hon?" asks the nurse.

"She awakes." From a rocking chair, Nick rises to stand next to me.

"You're here," I whisper.

"I'm here. How do you feel?"

I shake my head once. "Nasty. Bet I look nice."

The nurse finishes writing on her charts. "Be right back with some Tylenol. If you'd like."

I nod.

"I like your hair."

"Thanks. More professional, don't you think?"

"Especially with the bandages." Nick gazes at

me. "Beyond adorable."

Beyond adorable.

"Thanks for staying with me."

"I convinced your parents to go home. Said I was only going to stay for a short while in case you woke up. I mean, I knew you'd eventually wake up."

The hospital purrs with its steady and hushed sounds. I notice a glare on the lone picture on my hospital room wall. Grant Wood's *American Gothic*. I mention to Nick how I like the Grant Wood picture he gave his mom.

Shrugging, he says,"She doesn't seem to hate it." He points to *American Gothic*. "Do you like that one?"

"Gertrude Stein always said it reflected the small-mindedness of rural America."

"Who's Gertrude Stein?"

I giggle. "No one you'd probably care about."

"So," Nick says. "I heard you went to Omaha to think things out. Have you...made a decision?"

I take in a deep breath. "What do you think I should do?"

Staring directly at me he asks, "If both jobs were offered to you right here in Fox Plaine, which one would you choose?"

I sink into my hospital bed. I know the answer. But I don't wish to respond.

"Be honest."

"Hinkley."

His head drops. He begins to pick at his finger nails.

"Then you should go to Chicago."

I stop breathing, feeling my head begin to pitch. Chicago. It's too far. My stomach writhes. I put my hands over my face.

Nick gently takes my hands into his. "You need to go. You have to go."

In my quavery voice I ask, "Did they get my purse out of the car?"

"I think so," Nick says softly, looking around. Once he finds it, he sets it on my lap. I rummage in my bag through my watery eyes to find the photo.

Nick takes the picture and smiles with melancholy.

"You can't stay here, resenting what you do for the rest of your life."

"I love you Nick."

"We're in la la stage right now. That doesn't last forever."

"I can work in Omaha and live in Loam County. It's only an hour drive."

"You don't have such a great driving record."

"So you want me to go?"

Nick kisses my bandaged head. "I want you to be happy."

CHAPTER 55
TAKE A CHANCE

SEPTEMBER 1993

"Too much?" Jean asks as she jaunts into the bedroom decked out in her Chicago Cubs attire. Cubbie Visor. Cubbie Sunglasses. Cubbie Tank shirt. Cubbie Boxer shorts. Cubbie socks. Even her tennis shoes are bright blue.

"It's not right," I say all curled up on the bed.

She looks down at her outfit. "But you've never seen the crowd at Wrigley. I'll blend just fine."

"Not what I mean."

Nick should be going to this game with me.

Plowing in next to me, she says. "You've been moping for too long now. This is not the Amy Gaer I know. The Amy Gaer I know would be annoying the shit out of me with her chirpy singing."

I rub my temples.

"Look," she says with a sigh, "I can only be

the compassionate friend for so long. I know your misery is no fault of mine or this awesome city. It's about time you snap out of it."

I force a smile. Then I turn to her, sitting cross-legged on the bed. "I really am sorry. There are times I think I'm doing fine, then shit. I see a family and thoughts of Nick just eat me up." I feel my face go flush. "Maybe I am meant to be a small town girl. And I'm meant to be with him."

Putting her hand to my mouth she says, "Please don't sing that song. *I was born in a small town.* You know the one?"

"It's called Little Pink Houses. And I don't feel like singing."

Jean starts tapping her chin. "When I was lonely here, I threw myself into my work. Maybe you should do the same. I probably don't need to drag you to so many bars. It was sort of my way of breaking you into the city. And getting your mind off things."

"Everything you're doing for me has been really nice. But it's like someone's knocking on the door, and I can't decide if I want to let them in, even though I know I should."

"Well, for fuck sake. Let me in."

I nod. "I'll try. Harder." I look up at Jean. "But I need to tell you something else." She waves me on in her impatient sort of way. "I suck at my job."

"So, quit sucking at it."

"I can't help it. Every jingle I've written is so

bad. Apparently, I'm more of a performing type musician. Not so much the creating type. I seem to be good at one thing in the office. Making copies for the meetings."

"You're new. Still young. Give it some time. Maybe you're trying too hard."

Slamming my body back on the bed, I cover my face in shame. "I don't know. The other interns seem to be kicking ass, while I eat their creative dust. There's this one witch. Calls me Corny Pop."

"Corny Pop?"

"An attempt to be clever about my Iowa roots and my cliched pitches."

"Come on." She hops up. "I have a surprise for you before the game. I think it will perk you up."

"He hasn't even called me," I say staring at the phone in my room. "It's been three months." I don't tell Jean how many messages I've left him.

"Good," she says. "He wants to give you time."

I look at Jean and nod. "Apparently he didn't need any time."

***

"Why wouldn't you tell me this?" I whisper to Jean harshly, clutching her arm as she pours chips in a basket. I'm holding a tray of mimosas.

She cranes her neck out of the kitchen to check on her guests into the living room. Micah, the professor from the University of Chicago whom I met last winter in the bookstore, and his colleague Conrad are seated on her sofa and recliner discussing the upcoming game. Conrad seems to be making a statement with a Red Sox jersey.

Jean releases herself. "Don't be upset. I just want to help you move on." She pats me on the cheek. "I invited Micah when my turn with the company tickets came around. I told him I had six tickets, so if he knew of anyone else who might want to come, bring them along as well. I couldn't think of anyone else to invite."

I don't hesitate to offer her a stinky-eye before we enter the living room. And I'm even less happy with her when she takes the other chair, forcing me to sit on the sofa next to Micah. I ensure the space between us is at least the length of one arm so he won't get the wrong idea–although I'm quite certain that is Jean's intent. Jean and Micah didn't quite work out. Politics seemed to interfere with their attraction toward each other. So now she's going to spring him on me.

Dang.

He's definitely the doppelganger of Ethan Hawke.

I don't want to like anyone right now.

So my attention is focused on Micah's partner Conrad, whose spritely stature, dark hair, and dark beard give him an almost elfish appearance. Once I hear him speak, his Boston accent makes me envision him as a kid fighting on the streets. I can hardly imagine him a teacher of students. He looks more like the guy who'd be hanging out in dicey bar. But apparently, he's an anthropology professor.

"So, my students are writing essays on how Ruth Bader Ginsberg's appointment will have an impact on women's rights," offers Conrad, quickly switching from talk of baseball. "Of course, most of my class is supportive over the appointment. But initial discussions didn't yield much in the form of profound thoughts. My students don't really believe much more needs to be done— in the U.S. at least."

"Despite a palpable wage inequality?" asks Micah.

"You don't really understand until you actually experience it," I say. "I was shocked that gender issues even existed when I started working."

"No doubt," says Jean. "And it's not just a man versus woman issue. When I was promoted six months after my hire date, I faced just as much scrutiny from the women as the men. Maybe more. Rumors that I had slept around were started by women whom I thought were my friends."

"Uh, yeah, about that," I say. "I actually started that rumor."

My attempt at humor leaves them all speechless, and I feel a tiny bit small. Then Jean saves me with a, "I knew it. Crazy bitch." And the seriousness of the conversation shifts to a lighter note.

The more we talk, the closer Micah edges toward me with his animated hand gestures. Admittedly, he's engaging. I feel myself drawn into his clever talk. The buzz of the mimosas is making me feel more gregarious than I've felt in a long time. As a matter of fact, I feel a little buzzy. So I stand up and ask everyone if they need more drinks.

After refilling everyone's drinks, I make my way to the window to look over the view of Lake Michigan. Sailboats make their waves through the water as I sip on my tangy drink. Micah joins me and points out some of the swanky boats. When he mentions something about sailing sometime, I zone out and study his looks, wondering. Thinking. Then I notice his eyes really are nice. Almost sympathetic.

Then Micah says, "So you're a singer, I hear?"

"Karaoke style."

"We'll definitely need to hit a bar tonight then," he says. "Unless you want to sing for me now?"

This makes me laugh. "Just sing anything? Right now?"

"Why not?"

"Okay. See if you can guess this song. It's new. 'Twenty five years and my life is still–'"

"For a destination. Four Non-blondes. What's Up." Then he sings. I listen for a few verses. I can't stand not to sing this song. So I join him. And as we're singing, I connect to the vulnerability of the lyrics as a pit forms in my stomach. I barely notice the doorbell ringing as I wrap myself into the song. Jean goes to answer the door, and as I glance back to check out the next guest, I do a double take.

It's Nick.

Nick!

I hurdle through the living room, unable to fathom any proper courtesy.

"I'm guessing you know him?" Jean asks with her hands in the air.

Stumbling into the hallway, I put my hands on his chest before looking into his eyes. His very bloodshot eyes.

"I can't believe you're here," I say. "Not harvesting?"

He shakes his head, running his hand through his hair, which is somewhat flattened on one side. "It's raining at home."

"You don't look so well," I say. "Are you okay?"

"First time in a plane," he says.

"And?"

"I think I have a date with an eighty-six year old grandma."

He scratches his chin, looking around. Then he points to my T-shirt. "Already a Cubs fan?"

"I have tickets to my first game today!" I say with a flushed smile. But he just nods at me, staring. Already I feel an awkwardness between us. "I can't believe you're here. Why didn't you call?"

His eyes roll back as he puts his other hand behind his head.

"For starters, I got really fucked up with Will, Jake, and Penny last night." He looks down at me. "It seemed like a great idea to go after you. Last night. I haven't really slept. Now I'm feeling kind of stupid."

He looks toward the door. "Maybe I should go. You seem busy."

"What?" I say. "You come all the way to Chicago and now you're gonna go?"

"I don't know what I'm doing," he says. "Penny said I should go after you, but it's not like I want you to quit your job for me. And it's not like I can just move here. Or commute."

"Nick," I say grabbing his hands. "I'm kind of miserable. I've called you like, a bazillion and three times."

He lets go of my hands, then collapses against the wall. He shakes his head. "You don't look very miserable."

"I'm not creating ads. Good ones anyway. My stomach hasn't stopped hurting and I'm really pissed you won't call me back."

Staring at me with seemingly measured blinks, he lets out a long sigh.

"That's really great to hear." Drawing toward me, he brushes my bangs from my forehead. "Because...you know I'd move the farm here if I could. Maybe I should figure something else out. Get a job in construction or something."

"I want to come home," I say.

He folds me into him. "Do you really hate your job?"

I nod.

"God does answer prayers."

"I'm coming home."

"I won't stop you."

Just as I wrap my legs around him and we really start kissing, the door flies open. Jean clears her throat to ask, "Would you two like to join the party in here?"

I pull Nick into the apartment, introducing him to Conrad and Micah. Nick looks to me with raised eyebrows. "I interrupted something here, didn't I?"

Everyone is quiet as Jean pours Nick a mimosa which he tries to decline. Then Jean says, "So Nick I hear you're a baseball fan."

Nick shrugs. "Sorta."

"Cubs fan?"

"Sorry, no."

"You probably don't deserve my extra ticket then?"

"Nonsense," says Micah. "Wrigley field will convert him."

"Laughable," says Conrad. "Didn't convert me. Of course, I grew up with the Green Monster."

"I'll bet him by the end of the game he'll be converted," says Jean.

"Would it be possible to lose that bet?" says Nick.

"Only if he actually became converted," says Micah. "And admitted it."

***

Before we leave for the game Nick is tasked to

shower while Jean and I check ourselves in the bedroom. Jean turns to me. "Okay."

"Okay, what?"

"I get it," she says. "When you two look at each other. It's kind of sickening. And what he did? Flying out here? Pretty freaking romantic."

"I have to go back. I can find another job."

Jean puts her arm around me. "I thought if you came here, I wouldn't be so lonely. You're kind of like the sister I never had. Maybe never wanted really." She smiles. "But it's no fun living with a broody, love-sick roommate. Take your three-legged pigs and get back home. Wait." She turns to me. "Did you even bring your three-legged pigs?"

No. I left them at home.

CHAPTER 56

A HOUSE IN THE MIDDLE OF THE STREET

NOVEMBER 1993

"You about ready to move out of your parents' house now that you're like, what? Twenty-three or something?" Nick fumbles with a key to a house.

"And start making house payments?"

I pretend to be reluctant. But I still have my grandma's seed money held back, waiting for just the right investment to come along.

Nick is showing me a house on the edge of Perling. He has asked me a number of times if I plan to move to Omaha, near my job at First National Bank where I drive daily as an astute trainee in their loan officer program.

We enter the two-story house. Small oak pillars salute us in the foyer. And as we enter the living area to our right, I'm greeted by a wide, open staircase. I'm drawn to feel the woodwork, which is as smooth and soft as baby powder.

"High ceilings," I say loudly, shouting up in attempt to hear an echo. "HELLO HOUSE!"

The walls are texturized, painted bright white and makes for a cheery ambience. The gold carpets in the living area are worn, acutely in need of an update. But when we step into the kitchen, we are walking on a weathered wooden floor, and I'm reminded of the quaint Irish pubs I'd frequent in Iowa City.

"What do you think?" he asks.

"It's not too bad, I suppose." I pause. "Actually, it's pretty awesome. How much?"

"A steal. He'd even sell it on contract for a negotiable price." Nick stands with his arms folded. "Did you happen to glance into the office room? Over there?"

I trot to where Nick is pointing. I gasp.

A piano. A beautiful, old oak upright.

"It comes with the house."

I twinkle a few keys, which surprise me by being in tune.

"Own my own house, that comes with a piano?" I look out the window. "Oh look! A garden in the backyard! With a picket fence. Badly in need of a painting. But a picket fence!"

"There's something else I want you to see."

Nick pulls me up the staircase. Three bedrooms and a large closet in the hallway comprise the upstairs. We investigate each room, surveying the large bedroom last. The sun blasts brilliantly through the windows. Only a few dead flies rest between the sills. A few are doing their best to awaken.

I'm looking at a view of the church steeple when Nick asks, "Think this would be a great place to start a family?"

I glance at him questioningly.

He prances to the other side of the room. "Look in this closet."

He points to a small hidden door on the lower left side of the closet.

"What do you suppose that's for?" he asks.

I kneel down to turn the tiny knob, but it's locked. "Apparently it's for hiding contraband," I say, wondering if we'll really find any old remnants of a bootlegger's bounty. Nick reaches over me and attempts the lock.

"There must be a key around here somewhere." Nick is determined to open the door. As I crawl out of his way, he continues to search the closet.

"I found it! I found a key."

I return quickly as he grinds the key in the lock. He looks back at me, "You ready for this?"

"Just open it."

It sticks a little, but eventually opens. We kneel to look in the small aperture which is covered in pink, quilted satin.

"Fancy contraband."

In the middle sits a small black pouch. We look at each other, as if to challenge, then both grab for the pouch. But he beats me.

"What in the world?" I ask anxiously.

"Split it with you 50/50?"

"It's not really ours to keep."

He slowly brings it around, staring at the black box he's holding. Then he looks up and asks, "Will you marry me?"

"What?" I ask, unbalanced by the question.

"Will you marry me?" he asks again. "I found this house for us to live together. For us to buy."

"Are you asking for real?"

"Naw. I'm just kidding around." He shakes his head and drops the box. "Of course, I'm asking you for real. I didn't go through all this trouble for shits and giggles!"

I swallow, looking at the box he's holding. I can't believe what's happening!

"What about living on the farm? Don't you need to live there?"

He shakes his head.

"I can rent out the house. I want to start fresh. And I know how you always wanted to live in the city. I thought Perling would be a decent compromise."

"Absolutely," I say turning to him. "In that case, yes. My answer is yes!"

I clobber him with kisses as he tries to hold out his velvet pouch. He's smiling, wide. His eyes sparkle. "I'm trying to give you something."

The ring! He's trying to give me a ring.

"For you."

I place my hand in the pouch, but it doesn't feel like a ring. I remove the jewelry to find a necklace made of individual jade stones, strung together like a pearl necklace.

"It's beautiful."

"My godfather instructed me to give this to the love of my life. I found her."

I'm touched. I'm overwhelmed. It's a moment I don't want to end.

"You're quiet. Are you upset it's not a ring?" he asks. "I thought we could pick that out together. Consider this your engagement present."

"I'm not upset. I'm so entirely happy."

I throw my arms around Nick again. "Help me put this on. It'll look great with my Def Leppard concert t-shirt."

As Nick wraps the jewels around me, I realize he is making me a part of his history. And he is becoming a part of mine. Nothing seems more natural right now. I'm the love of his life. He is the love of mine.

We are nestled in the closet, and he tells me the story of his uncle. It's the first of many stories we will share. As I'm listening to Nick, it occurs to me how complete I feel when we're together. I can't imagine us not plotting and planting our history here, in the county where we both grew up.

We'll visit many places and do many things together, but it's not money or grandeur that will make our lives fulfilling. No matter what we do or where we go, even in a closet, sharing stories, we are happy. I am happy. It's just that simple.

Present Day

My daughter has wandered over to me.

"Too many songs?" she asks. "Got a little carried away once I started."

I lift myself up, wrapping my arms around her.

"I'm ready for my critique," she says. "What could I do better?"

I squeeze her tighter.

"Nothing. It was perfect."

"No performance is perfect, Mom."

Admittedly, my heart has lightened as I let my memory wander with my daughter's music transcending me beyond the present. And just as my daughter pulls away, continuing on how she needs to improve her pitch on the low notes, my husband announces himself through the door–only to be attacked by his two little minions.

For the first time in a long time, I take a moment to watch him with his brood. He's bronzed, a bit grimy, and still quite sculpted from his days working on the farm. I believe my heart has even just skipped.

"Sorry, running late. I'd sure hate to be late for the Biebs tonight."

"One Direction, but nice try," I say with a

wink. "I think you were trying to miss it."

Tilting his head as one boy crawls up his back and one crawls up his leg he asks, "You wearing those jeans?"

I glance down. "You don't like?"

He nods. "I do. Really. It's nice how you match Marra. Is that the fashion these days? Mother-daughter outfits?"

And then something happens that hasn't occurred in a long time. We laugh. Together. I actually laugh so hard I cry.

"You're in a good mood," he says.

The comment makes me sad. "You mean for a change?" He shakes his head, as if to avoid an argument. I waddle over to him in my tight pants and offer a hug. "I love you."

He pulls my head back to see my teary eyes. "I love you too. Are you okay?"

"I'm sorry. For being so crabby all the time. I just... remembered. This is everything I want."

Nick hugs me tightly while the boys clamor. My daughter tiptoes up behind and throws herself around us.

"We're just busy right now," he whispers. "Try not to worry so much about stuff." He steps back. "And I like it that you put those jeans on. Really. Apparently they made you relax a little. Maybe you should wear them to the concert."

Simultaneously, my daughter and I say, "No."

"I'm gonna change," I say. Then I start instructions. "Nick, you hop in the shower. Marra, please wash up your brothers. I'll try to peel these jeans off. Everyone to the Explorer in fifteen."

***

Our concert experience is chaos.

Quinn pukes a blue icey.

Cole cries over getting the wrong T-shirt.

And Marra pouts because we leave the concert early, complaining vociferously about how she was forced to attend the concert of her lifetime with her family.

But Nick and I hold hands on the way home, as we travel back from Omaha to the farm, commenting on how we wished it would've been a Black Keys concert. Maybe next time we could attend something we really want to see by ourselves. Maybe.

I glance behind me to see my three children, who are now dozing off despite the *Brave* DVD playing. The LCD glare makes them *appear* all cherubic and perfect. I'm not saying they're not perfect and cherubic. They really are. Especially when they're dozing. Marra is wearing my butterfly pin on her jacket. The girl's got style. Obviously. Look at those jeans.

Nick switches on the iPod to Norah Jones. Then he turns to me.

"Sing to me?"

"Over Norah?"

"You don't sing enough anymore," he says.

As I begin to hum, Nick lifts my fingers to kiss them, whispering, "Beyond adorable."

Once the song is over Nick asks, "Ever think about pulling back a bit? At work, I mean?" He pauses for a moment. In a quieter voice he adds, "Maybe you should quit to do something less stressful."

"What?" I ask. "I'm like the president now, Nick." I shake my head. "I can't just give up the salary. Or quit on the staff at Loam State."

"Other people can run banks. I think we can afford it."

"But I'm a woman," I say. "How's that gonna look? Like the woman banker couldn't cut it?"

"I didn't say stay at home and do nothing."

Letting go of his hand, I lean into the window. "What would I do?"

"What would make you happy?" he asks. "Really happy?"

I'm humming again, thinking. Music. Music makes me happy.

The piano begins on the next Norah song, weaving a few well-placed harmonies into my ear. "And how do you propose I turn music into a career?"

Grabbing my hand again, he says, "I didn't say anything about turning music into a career. I'm not proposing anything. I just worry about how happy you are at times."

The velvety voice of Norah melds into the jazzy piano, throwing me into some place between tranquility and hope. I close my eyes and visions begin to swim in my mind. Voice lessons for kids. Community theater. An interactive music store. The visions expand into more family time. More living. Sitting up straighter, I turn to Nick and say "Maybe."

"Maybe, what?"

"I'll consider something different. Maybe I could give music lessons." I look back at the kids. "Or just stay home to teach our kids."

I take the harmony part of the song. A tear manages its way out. The lyrics I sing are meaningless. But the music in my belly has everything to do with what I've done in my life. My career. How my career has often left me burned out and sometimes neglectful of my family. Did the money and status make me turn a blind eye to what's important?

Maybe.

Not completely. My career also made me who I am. I can hardly regret the opportunities it has afforded me–afforded us. And I like to think I've made an impact on lives. In the companies I worked. Within our community. But now the thought of stepping back and perhaps venturing into one of my greatest passions excites me beyond words.

Caressing my cheek Nick says, "No need to cry. Just sing."

Shifting to face my family who now has awakened to the music, I do just that.

I sing. And no matter what I decide to do, I will keep on singing.

Made in the USA
Monee, IL
14 August 2024